HANK J. KIRBY

HANGTREE
COUNTY

Complete and Unabridged

LINFORD
Leicester

First published in Great Britain in 2010 by
Robert Hale Limited
London

First Linford Edition
published 2011
by arrangement with
Robert Hale Limited
London

British Library CIP Data

Kirby, Hank J.
  Hangtree County. - -
  (Linford western library)
  1. Brothers- -Fiction. 2. Revenge- -Fiction.
  3. Western stories. 4. Large type books.
  I. Title II. Series
  823.9'2–dc22

ISBN 978–1–4448–0914–5

Published by
F. A. Thorpe (Publishing)
Anstey, Leicestershire

Set by Words & Graphics Ltd.
Anstey, Leicestershire
Printed and bound in Great Britain by
T. J. International Ltd., Padstow, Cornwall

This book is printed on acid-free paper

HANGTREE COUNTY

Drew Hardy always found himself overshadowed by his brothers, Kerry and Luke. Then he was jailed for attempted murder. Four years later, a twist of fate sets him free. But would freedom mean working for Kerry and Luke whilst they ensured he never got his share of the family ranch? He must settle the matter with guns — time in jail had taught him plenty about those. Now, for the first time, Drew was a force to be reckoned with.

1

Mavericks

No one had any idea the kid was so handy with a six-gun until the day he killed the halfbreed Mexican who called himself 'Quitar' — the Remover.

It was in a canyon in the Sierra Diablos, known locally as Busted Leg.

Emmett Hardy and his youngest son, Drew, headed up a herd of some seventy mavericks they and the two drag riders had rounded-up in the Diablos these last two weeks. It was damned hard work, popping those mean-eyed sons of bitches out of the brush, and the Lazy H men had lost plenty of sweat — not to mention hide — doing it.

They had penned them in a small box canyon to let them calm down and get used to crowding together — mavericks

1

were essentially loners and suspicious ones at that.

It was anybody's guess how they would behave on the trail back to Lazy H, north-west of Van Horn, but Emmett figured the four of them could handle it without much trouble.

And they might have done if Jesse Kinane and his bunch hadn't stretched across Pinchnose Pass, with rifle butts on their thighs and mean-eyed looks that boded no good at all for the Lazy H crew.

Quitar sat a few feet distant from Jesse's men, hands folded on his saddle horn, swarthy skin gleaming with a film of sweat not yet dulled by settling dust — which told Emmett they had been waiting in the rocks and had just ridden out to block the way when they saw the cranky mavericks butting and bawling their way through the pass. The breed was a big man with a thick black moustache beneath his nose which had yawning nostrils, now flared in anticipation of action.

And the action that Quitar liked was laced with gunsmoke — and blood.

Emmett Hardy lifted a hand, signalling the drag riders to hold the herd while he dealt with this — whatever it was. Though he had a pretty good idea it was an attempt at hijacking the mavericks. Drew, fair-haired, slim and still a little gawky at eighteen, almost nineteen, years, set his roan alongside his father's although Emmett glowered.

'Stay back, boy.'

'My place is beside you, Pa.'

'When you're growed some more. This might get kinda nasty and — '

'Them's my steers, Hardy,' called Jesse Kinane, a lean, humourless man in his forties, with prominent cheekbones that gave his face a sunken look around the mouth now the sun threw deep shadows from almost directly above.

'Funny, never seen you sweatin' an' cussin' an' losin' a little hide out there in the Diablos the last coupla weeks. My boys, sure, not you — nor any of your crew.'

3

'No need. Them's my steers.'

'Don't see no brand on 'em — but if I did, they wouldn't be mavericks, would they? And mavericks are free for the takin' for any man who can do it on open range.'

Jesse spat. 'See, that's your problem. That ain't open range where you throwed your rope. That's part of my land — and shared with some of these boys you might recognize from out of our little basin.'

'Yeah — I noted you was all nesters.'

'Not nesters — *settlers*! That's how it's writ on the prove-up papers. You wanta argue that, you gonna have a Ranger in your lap with a warrant in one hand, gun in the other.'

Emmett lifted his sweat-stained curl-brim hat, and sniffed loudly as he scratched at his thinning string-coloured hair. 'Well, I don't care to have no truck with Rangers.'

Jesse's craggy face moved in a smug smile. 'I reckoned not. But seein' as you've brung them mavericks outta the

Diablos, we'll relieve you of 'em and split 'em among us for our spreads. No sense in drivin' 'em back — or turnin' 'em loose again.'

Emmett glanced at Drew, saw the young cowboy seemed relaxed enough in the saddle, right hand resting idly on his thigh. But there was a touch of tightness about his mouth and eyes that brought a frown to Emmett's face. 'Easy now, boy. We'll handle this OK.'

'Quitar's hoping you won't,' Drew murmured, his words surprising his father.

The rancher glanced at the big breed, saw the kid was right. Quitar's broad shoulders were tensed like a plank, the knotted muscles showing through his tight grey shirt. His tongue kept wetting his lips under the heavy moustache, but Emmett reckoned it wasn't nervousness making him do it — it was eagerness to use his six-gun, which was set for a cross-draw, angled just right, butt big and ugly, easy to get a good grip on in a hurry.

And those dark beads of eyes were fairly burning with anticipation. *He was impatient for a killing.*

'Since when you hire cheap gunnies, Jesse? We've never gone head-to-head so bad as to need that.'

Kinane spat and smiled crookedly. He gestured to the unsmiling horsemen either side of him. 'We've formed a Settlers' Alliance, Emmett. Strength and power in numbers. Reckon you know that, with that big crew you got on Lazy H, not to mention your three boys, ready to back you up.'

Emmett nodded slowly. 'Flexin' some muscle, huh? Well, you picked the wrong day for it, Jesse. I'm ready to expand, got more range under title down along the Rio Concho, and now I need cows to fill it and start breedin'.'

The nesters murmured, moved restlessly: obviously they hadn't known the Hardys were expanding legally.

Jesse Kinane's lips tightened. 'By hell, that don't set good with us, Hardy! You got half the county as it is.'

'Legally so. All registered with the Land Commissioner. You got no claim to these mavericks, Jesse. So just move aside and let us through.'

Kinane was silent, nostrils flaring. The breed hardcase was looking slantwise at him, trying to keep an eye on Emmett and Drew at the same time.

'Jus' say the word, *amigo*.'

'Consider it said, Quitar!' snapped Kinane and there wasn't a man there who didn't jump or jerk or gasp as two gunshots roared and slapped back from the narrow walls of the pass — and Quitar was punched back in an untidy roll over the rump of his prancing mount. He hit in a cloud of dust, sprawled on his back, his face a mess of blood, more red glistening just below his throat.

'Judas priest!' Kinane exclaimed, wide-eyed, his voice cracking as he fought his own restless mount.

Like everyone else there, he was staring at Drew Hardy — and the smoking Colt Drew held in his right

7

hand, the hammer already cocked for a third shot if it seemed necessary.

'Hey, Jesse!' called one of the nesters who had dismounted to kneel by the dead hardcase. His voice was quavery and he glanced nervously at Drew. 'Quitar's gun — it's still in leather!'

It was true. The breed's gun had never left its holster despite his attempt at his usual fast draw.

'No one's that fast!' Jesse said, his breath coming in short gasps, betraying his shock. 'Sure not agin someone with Quitar's reputation!'

'He went for his gun,' Drew said in a surprisingly steady voice. 'When I shot and he jarred back and twisted the way he did, he must've rammed it back in the holster — reflex action. He couldn't've moved it more'n a couple of inches from leather before I fired.'

There was silence, broken only by the stomping of one of the horses, the swishing of tails as flies buzzed.

Jesse Kinane was white about the mouth but he bared his teeth and said with a certain satisfaction, 'You might get to keep them mavericks, Hardy — but you won't get to keep that murderin' son of yours!' He pointed a shaking gnarled finger at the kid. 'I'm gonna see him hang for this!'

'You're loco!'

Jesse shook his head confidently. 'He already had his gun out, down at his side, away from us: *must've!* No other way he coulda done it! Shot Quitar cold! We got plenty of witnesses! An', by the way' — he gestured to a small man on his left — 'Josh Cameron's youngest son just got betrothed to Judge Lacy's second daughter last Sunday. How you reckon we'll do when this gets to court, Hardy?'

Emmett's weary face was set in hard lines now. He saw Drew was edgy beside him and glanced behind as the mavericks bawled and jostled. The drag men were riding around, coiled ropes at the ready, anxious now the beasts were nervous after the shooting.

'Well, Jesse, I ain't sure how you'll go

in court — but I was you, I'd sure as hell go *now!*' He hipped in the saddle and called loudly. 'Careful, boys! Them cows look to me like they're ready to break 'n run — and Jesse and his pards here are right smack in the way!' He whipped off his old hat and let out a wild rebel yell and the drag men got the message, ran their mounts into the rear of the herd, ropes slapping dust from rough hides.

It startled the mavericks there and they surged forward, horns jabbing, and in seconds the herd was up and running. Emmett and Drew reined aside, climbed their mounts up the scant cover of the slopes of soil and rock, wind-built, at the base of the pass walls. There was just enough room for the cattle to surge past without the horns ripping into their mounts stomping on the barely adequate footing.

'Pa, watch out!'

Drew called wildly and his six-gun came around blazing, as Jesse Kinane brought his rifle to his shoulder, shooting even as he tried to wheel his horse aside. He got off one shot, and the bullet sounded like an angry bee going past Emmett Hardy's face. Then Jesse reeled in the saddle and his rifle fell. He instinctively snatched for it and tumbled out of leather. His boot caught in the stirrup as the wild-eyed mount raced away from the stampede.

It saved his life, though it beat the hell out of him for ten yards or so, his body bouncing and banging off the ground and rocks as the horse took the line of least resistance and cleared the pass in time to swing aside from the surge of bawling mavericks.

As the dust boiled around them and they fought to keep their mounts on the narrow strips of raised ground, Emmett, white-faced now, said to Drew,

'You saved my life, boy! Twice!'

Drew grinned, six-gun in holster now. 'Pleasure, Pa.'

'Dammit, boy — where you learn to shoot a Colt like that?'

Drew coughed in the dust, had to

shout. 'When you sent me on them lone line shack deals, and outridin' to the spreads, looking for any of our beeves that had wandered, I sort of practised, shootin' at branches and cans and stones — you know, something to fill in the time. I got to like it.'

'Well, no one on my side of the family was ever much good with a pistol — rifle, yeah — and I know you're a fine shot with a Winchester or Sharps — but the way you nailed that breed!' Then he sobered. '*Did* you have the gun out, down at your side where they couldn't see it?'

Drew, eyes reddened from the glare and dust, looked squarely at his father. 'No, Pa — I just went for it when I seen Quitar making his move. That's gospel.'

Emmett nodded slowly. 'Well, I reckon we're gonna have a mighty tough time provin' that to Judge Lacy if his son's gonna marry one of them nester women. I mean, no one even seen you do anythin' like that before.'

Drew shrugged, then said, 'Kerry and

Luke did — once. They come to relieve me up at the Tomcat Ridge line camp and I was blazing away at a row of empty bottles. They seen me, but Kerry just said, 'You better not let Pa know you been practisin' with a six-shooter like that or he'll bend it over your head.''

'Kerry said that?'

Drew nodded. 'Luke backed him up. That's why I never let on. I just seem to have a natural fast draw, I guess. Never figured I'd have to use it, like I did with Quitar.'

Emmett found himself thinking about his other two sons: Kerry, the eldest and most bitter, and Luke, the one who walked in Kerry's shadow. Neither got on well with Drew — figured he was favoured by Emmett, not only for being the youngest, but because his mother — Emmett's second wife, Eve, a fortyish, flaxen-haired widow from Santa Fe — had died giving birth to Drew and — Emmett had to admit it — he *did* favour the youngster. Couldn't help it. After nearly twenty years he still felt an aching emptiness for Eve. Drew had his mother's looks, especially her eyes and her flaxen hair, many of her mannerisms and a lot of her temperament. He regarded the boy as being all that he had left of Eve and, perhaps selfishly, did all he could to nurture and perpetuate that feeling . . .

He had known it would cause friction with Kerry and Luke, but his second marriage had already done that, anyway. He figured he could handle it, even though they had a heap of his own cussedness in them. But — you could never tell when a 'but' was going to jump out and rear up and bite you — but the older boys showed real resentment and treated Drew mighty mean at times . . . with a jealousy that was close to genuine hatred . . .

Emmett had taken them to task but guilt kept him from being as tough and straight with them as he ought to have been so as to end it quickly. He was used to laying down the law on Lazy H and expected to be obeyed. But this situation somehow seemed different: he admitted to himself he had underestimated it, let it get out of hand — and now it was too late to change things.

It had crept up on him, and he had failed to notice just how hostile and wounded his two elder sons felt. Josie, their mother, Emmett's first wife, had been plain and humourless and had kept a tight rein on both boys until she died suddenly, washing clothes. She just folded forward and buried her head in a tub of suds and dirty Levis. And just after she was buried, he had had the chance to get his hands on some of the best rangeland in the county because a railroad had overrun the deadline for settlement: they had overextended their finances, needed ready cash for some other, more urgent project — and Emmett was able to find that money . . .

He had been mighty pleased with himself, pulling off that deal, *mighty* pleased. It would make Lazy H a ranch to be reckoned with in Hangtree County, West Texas.

But now he wondered if he shouldn't have spent less time on buttering-up banks and lawyers and tried harder to smooth over the thorny situation that had developed between his three sons.

Emmett Hardy was a man who believed in hunches, had followed them most of his life — and now that Drew had mentioned that Kerry and Luke were the only witnesses to his phenomenal speed with a six-shooter, he felt a familiar uncomfortable knotting in his belly.

A hunch that, if Jesse Kinane followed through with his threat to go to court over the shootings, he was going to find out just how big his mistake might have been in favouring Drew over the other boys.

2

Boot Hill

Thunderheads, steely blue and purple, reared over the town of Hangtree on the day of Emmett Hardy's funeral four years later.

There was a big crowd, because Emmett, for all his cantankerousness and rough ways, had been a generous man to the town and the county itself. Of course, there was a good percentage of mourners who came only because they were glad to see old Emmett interred in the Texas soil he loved: some had even offered to dig the grave a couple of feet deeper to make sure the old bastard *stayed* buried.

But there were no real disruptions, only hoarsely whispered disparaging remarks here and there as the preacher read the burial service, and threw in a brief eulogy, included in his already more-than-adequate funeral fee.

There was just one big disturbance, though: when, almost at the end of Preacher Dodd's reading, Drew Hardy arrived — running late and wearing handcuffs, flanked by two deputy wardens from Hudspeth Penitentiary.

Silence fell over the town's Boot Hill like a dropped blanket. All eyes turned to the trio as they came panting up the slope to the grave site, atop the rise.

Not many would have recognized Drew Hardy, remembering him only as the gawky kid with the ready smile and long flaxen hair with its natural waves causing it to fall over his right eye: the kid some called the 'Fastest Gun Alive' and who had used that gun to kill a nester — *settler* — and wound another, four years before . . .

Those flaxen locks were long gone, his hair cropped close to his skull. There was a deep scar about three inches long over the right eye now, and the smile was absent. Lips that seemed to have thinned over these past four years, gave his face a hard, wary look with flinty eyes either side of a nose that had been broken and badly set: prison doctors were not noted for their finesse or devotion to the finer points of their profession.

He wore a plain denim shirt, faded, but looking clean enough, though a little crumpled. He held a battered curl-brim hat in his hands, but it failed to hide the manacles. His trousers were denim, also, patched on one hip, cuffs frayed over scratched and dusty, clumsy boots.

The deputies were sober, big men, but one a few years older than his companion. His name was Grissom: the younger, meaner-looking guard was called Hume.

Grissom removed his hat and nodded to the preacher. 'Sorry we're late, preacher — stage bogged down at the creek crossin'.'

The man of the cloth cleared his throat, nodding in curt acceptance of the apology. 'We will continue then . . . '

'How come he's here at all?'

The voice came from the front row of mourners, across the grave from where Drew and the guards stood.

The speaker was around six feet, shoulders stretching his dark blue shirt, dark hair slicked back with water or pomade: hard to tell from this distance. He had a square-jawed face, clean-shaven but not very well, and hard, hard eyes as they looked directly at Drew.

'Knew you'd be glad to see me, Kerry,' Drew said to his oldest brother. Then he flicked his gaze to the slim man, beside Kerry Hardy, just as tall but slimmer and with a pointed, slightly receding jaw. 'How about you, Luke? Got a welcome for your kid brother?'

'No — But I'll say *adios* quick enough.'

Drew smiled thinly, glanced at Grissom. 'They're just joshin' — can't wait for me to do my other three years in Hudspeth and come back and work

Lazy H with 'em.'

Kerry's face didn't change. 'Sure, do your three years, Drew, but don't bother comin' back.'

'No, nothin' for you at Lazy H,' added Luke a mite smugly.

'See? They like to josh.'

Hume nudged Drew hard in the ribs with his elbow, addressed the preacher. 'You'd best finish-up, deacon — we gotta get this one back to Hudspeth soon as we can.'

The minister cleared his throat, frowning, not pleased that the service had been interrupted. The crowd was murmuring restively, too, as the droning voice continued with the traditional burial service . . .

Drew's head was bowed but his gaze roved around the mourners. *Good turn-out*, he thought, *must be half the town*. Some looked bored, obviously there because they figured they should show their faces, even if their sympathy was transparently hypocritical.

He picked out a young woman in a

grey bonnet, trimmed with sky-blue, and wearing a dress of the same colour that stood out amongst the more traditional black. He caught her eye and was about to mouth some words at her when he was aware the preacher had reached '*Ashes to ashes, dust to dust . . .*'

Grissom nudged him gently. 'Go ahead, boy.'

Hume grunted sourly but Drew shuffled forward and awkwardly picked up a double handful of West Texas soil, shuffled to the graveside and let it trickle down on to the coffin in the bottom of the pit. He stood for a moment, as if trying to see through the varnished wood with its silver plaque in the shape of a scroll to where his father lay on the padded, ruffled silk inside.

'Sorry I couldn't make it in time to see you, Pa.'

He was shouldered roughly aside and he snapped his head around, eyes narrowed and blazing. Kerry stepped back, startled by the murderous look on his young brother's face, his breath hissing through his teeth.

Drew grinned suddenly. 'Sorry, big brother — instinctive reaction. You don't let anyone jostle you in the pen without showin' your resentment.'

Kerry swallowed. 'Go back to the rockpile — an' stay there!'

'I will — for three years, mebbe a little less if I'm a good boy. But I'll be back.'

'You'll be plumb loco if you are.'

'Gentlemen! *Please!*' The preacher was aghast. 'Such behaviour on a solemn occasion like . . .'

Hume pulled Drew back roughly and shoved him away from the grave. Kerry sneered slightly, sprinkled in the earth and dropped to one knee in a silent, short prayer at the edge of the grave. Luke joined him a few moments later, and then the mourners who had been respectfully waiting for the family to pay their last respects, started forward in a slow-moving line, many glancing apprehensively at Drew.

Hume started to drag Drew away, but he resisted. 'Just a minute, someone I want to speak to.'

'What you want won't gimme a moment's sleeplessness, mister! We're leavin' — now!'

Grissom stepped in front of Hume. 'We've got plenty of time before the stage leaves. Let him have a minute.'

Hume glared. 'Warden said he was to be here no more'n a *few* minutes.'

'They ain't up yet, by my count.' Grissom spoke flatly, a man in his fifties with a paunch that meant he had to wear his belt quite low under the bulge. Whether by accident or design, his big right hand rested on the butt of his holstered Colt.

Hume glared, muscles knotting on his jaw as he gritted his teeth. He nodded jerkily. 'You're in charge. But the warden ain't gonna like this, when I tell him.'

'I won't like it, either — when you tell him.' Grissom's bleak look changed to a warmer one as he turned to Drew.

'Who you want to see, Drew?'

Drew pointed with a tilting motion of his stubbled jaw.

'The woman in the grey-an'-blue? Aw, she's comin' over anyway. Be quick, Drew.'

'Thanks, Grissom.'

As the guard stepped away, taking the scowling Hume's arm and pulling him with him, Drew turned to the young woman. Dark hair spilled from beneath the bonnet and the reflected sunlight from the pale soil showed an oval face with a smile touching the small mouth, grey-green eyes crinkling slightly. She offered a grey-gloved hand.

'Glad you could make it, Drew.' Her voice was soft and easy on the ear.

'Wouldn't've if you hadn't tackled the warden in person, Lee — I thank you for it. No one even told me Pa had died.'

Lee Dekker frowned slightly, glanced towards Kerry and Luke where they stood near the preacher now, giving her hostile looks. 'Your brothers ought to be ashamed of themselves.'

'Reckon not.' Drew smiled. 'Was it a heart attack like they say? Warden claimed he didn't know details.'

'Yes, Dr Giles is satisfied. He'd been treating your father for his head injuries after that fall from his horse, but he's sure he died of heart failure.'

'I never knew — I don't get allowed mail.'

'What! Good heavens, that's not right! I-I did wonder why you hadn't answered my letters . . . '

'You wrote me?'

'Several times.' Colour suddenly burned in her cheeks. 'I — thought you might need a little — cheering-up.'

He shook his head. 'No.' Then, at her injured look he smiled. 'I needed a *lot* of cheerin'-up an' I'm sorry I missed your letters, Lee.'

'You'll be a damn sight sorrier you make us miss that stage!' growled Hume coming back and forcing himself between the prisoner and the woman. Lee staggered, her shoes catching on a clod of earth and stumbling. Drew tried to steady her but the manacles made it awkward. However, she managed to retain her balance.

Hume stepped in close, turning his back on her, grabbing Drew's arms in a painful grip. 'Let's go!'

Hume's eyes were on the same level as Drew's and he stepped back slightly as he saw the burning anger in the prisoner's blue stare. Then he gasped and doubled-up violently as Drew's knee rammed up between his legs. He sank to his knees and Drew kicked him in the shoulder before Grissom pulled him back.

'You damn fool! It'll be solitary for you when we get back! An' that'll be the least of your worries! You know how the warden feels about prisoners even raisin' a fist to the guards.'

Drew ignored him and steadied Lee. 'All right?'

She straightened her bonnet, nodding vigorously. 'Yes, I'm fine. But you — you've made some bad trouble for yourself, it seems.'

Drew said carelessly. 'Only kind of trouble they know in Hudspeth.'

'Drew, don't — joke about it — please!'

He was dragged away by Grissom then as Kerry and Luke helped Hume to his feet. Kerry grinned.

'Almost wish I was comin' back with you this time, little brother!'

'Not as much as I wish you were.'

Kerry scowled and Grissom dragged Drew Hardy away from the graveside, heading for the cemetery gates.

'Might be better you don't poke your nose into Lazy H business, Lee.'

She gave Kerry a cool look. 'Better for whom?'

'Guess,' he said curtly, striding away to where Luke stood waiting, not looking too sure of himself.

As always.

3

Hero

It was a big stagecoach, a nine-seater, with three rows of seats, and had travelled thousands of miles. Hand-built in 1867 by Abbott-Downing in New Hampshire, it was one of thirty coaches; Wells Fargo's largest single order for hand-built stagecoaches ever received by that prestigious factory.

So, although much of the United States had rolled beneath its iron-tyred wheels for a lot of years, and a lot of plump backsides had polished and worn away the leather seat coverings, it was still a very comfortable vehicle. Abbott-Downing were noted for their quality and attention to detail where the comfort of coach passengers was concerned.

Drew Hardy sat between Hume and

Grissom, and there was enough room so they weren't wedged together, had space to breathe and even move their arms. Hume crowded Drew anyway: he would have been happier if the prisoner had been slung between the axles down among the dust and grit kicked up by the six-horse team — he could hardly wait to get Hardy back within the walls of Hudspeth Penitentiary.

Grissom countered by moving closer to the end of the seat, giving Drew a shade more room to move his arms so he could draw on the cigarette Grissom had rolled for him. Even so, Hume managed to knock it from the prisoner's grip and laughed out loud at Drew's frantic efforts to get the burning cigarette out of his lap before it seared a hole in the cloth — and his skin beneath.

'You're a petty sonofabitch,' Grissom growled, keeping his voice low, not wanting to upset the other passengers. All seats were full: two men and four women of varying ages, all well dressed.

When boarding, Drew, clumsy with his hands cuffed in the small space, had knocked the wide-brimmed hat from the older woman, apologized, and contorted himself to stoop and retrieve it for her. She blinked in surprise and he heard her murmur to her male escort, 'Goodness! Manners — from a handcuffed prisoner!'

Hume had snorted, and now said roughly after the cigarette incident, 'We ain't here to give him comfort, Grissom! You better remember that.'

'I'll remember — and how you knocked the smoke from his hands. Miserable sonofa.'

Hume glared and his lips moved in a curse. Then he stomped on Drew's nearest instep and hooked a sharp elbow against the man's neck as he instinctively bent forward.

'Now that's enough!' snapped Grissom, his lashing voice stopping all conversation in the coach as it swayed towards the Diablos. 'I mean it, Hume!'

'Aaaah! You're not only soft-hearted,

you're soft-*headed*.'

'Get some sleep,' Grissom growled, then looked at Drew who was still wincing after the high heel had driven hard into his instep. 'OK?'

Hardy nodded, smiling crookedly. 'Ought still be able to walk by the time we get to Hudspeth.'

Grissom shook his head slowly. 'How you manage to keep your sense of humour?'

'Didn't know I had.' Hardy wriggled his buttocks a little, eased his back against the seat. 'Might take that advice you gave Hume and catch up on some shut-eye.'

'You do that, Hardy!' gritted Hume. ''Cause I'm gonna see you don't get much rest when we're back in the pen.'

The other passengers were clearly uncomfortable with a handcuffed prisoner riding with them, but, as one of the men said to his worried-looking wife, 'Just think how it might be if he *wasn't* cuffed, my dear.'

That brought another sudden silence,

except that one of the two young girls, in a checkered frock, giggled behind her hand, unable to stop, tossing slantwise glances at Drew.

But he was facing away and stretched out his legs, right instep throbbing, cuffed hands resting on his midriff. He closed his eyes, thinking about the funeral — and Emmett . . .

★   ★   ★

There had been an aftermath to that run-in with Jesse Kinane and his settlers. Drew still thought of them as nesters . . .

He had wounded Jesse when the man had raised his rifle, once again drawing and shooting with such speed that he was accused of having had the gun in his hand all the time, held down by his leg, out of sight of Kinane.

Although Jesse had been more badly injured by his tumble from his mount and being dragged, he made much of the shallow groove on his scalp left by

Drew's bullet grazing him. 'Meant to take my damn head off!'

Following-up on his threat to see Drew hang for killing Quitar — and making sure Judge Lacy was sitting on the bench — when in the witness box he accused the young cowboy of being a killer.

'He was ready and willin' to kill Quitar, Judge — Havin' his gun already out and waitin' proves that.'

'You're a liar.'

The judge, heavy-jowled with tousled grey hair, frowned as he banged his gavel solidly. 'The prisoner will not speak unless directly addressed!'

'Sure, Judge,' Drew said, 'and as you're addressin' me right now, I'd like to say again, Jesse Kinane is a liar and so is anyone else who reckons I had my gun out of leather before that breed started to reach for his hogleg — '

Half the sentence was spoken against the thudding of the wooden hammer on the gavel pad and the shouting of Kinane's lawyer and the judge, the tattoo of boots as the orderly hurried to where Drew stood in the dock.

After things had settled down, with Emmett frowning in his front row seat, flanked by his other two sons, the judge gestured to Kinane in the witness box to continue.

He did so, with more accusations of the same, more interruptions by Drew — Emmett and his boys were strangely silent — until at last Drew shouted,

'Dammit, Judge, let me prove it!'

Sudden silence. Judge Lacy, glaring, said, 'What?'

'Lemme show you I'm as fast as I claim, Judge. I ain't showin' off, fact I'm kinda nervous about it all, but it seems to be the only way this is gonna be settled.'

'Won't change nothin'!' snapped Kinane. 'You still killed Quitar!'

'But, if the boy can show he has such phenomenal gun speed, it will be self-defence,' said Drew's lawyer, some-one else who hadn't had a lot to say in his defence so far.

After a lot of argument, the judge agreed to repair to the rear in the court grounds, and set it up for Drew's demonstration.

Then it took only a few minutes for everyone who had crowded back there to believe Drew Hardy.

First he set up as targets empty whiskey bottles that were found piled in a corner of the yard — no one knew how they might have gotten there. In seconds none of them had a neck left on the spinning, broken bottle bodies.

Silence, as gunsmoke and gunshots rolled away into the hot blue Texas sky. Then Drew picked up two of the necks that hadn't totally shattered, tossed them into the air, drew and fired — he had to use four bullets but he hit one and had fired all four shots before they touched the ground. Kinane's lawyer didn't seem to think that was fast enough, so Drew asked the man to pick up the last intact bottle neck, hold it at his side, arm extended at waist level, then to let it drop.

'And what will that accomplish?' the man asked, suddenly a little pale and sweating.

'I'll hit it before it touches ground.'

'What! Falling less than two feet? You'll draw from your holster and hit that bottleneck?' The man shook his head. 'Can't be done — and I don't intend to be part of this — circus!'

That effectively got him off the hook, but there were some sniggers, and then Emmett strode forward, picked up the glass tube in question and stood with his back to the fence, holding it at arm's length, just below waist level.

'When you're ready, Drew.'

'Just let it drop, Pa.'

Emmett opened his fingers and jumped when there was an almost instantaneous shot and glass shards stung his left hip — luckily he was wearing leather chaps or he may have been cut.

'Did you have that gun down at your side all along?' asked the judge hoarsely, clearing his throat.

'You know I didn't, Judge — I'll do it again if I have to. Gotta admit I ain't always as accurate. 'Fact, hitting that neck just now was more of a fluke — but if I'd been aiming to shoot Jesse's head off, he'd be about ten inches shorter now.'

That got a few laughs and a scowl from Kinane. Judge Lacy nodded to the armed guards who had been keeping loaded rifles trained on Drew while he conducted his exhibition. 'We'll return to the court room — I believe the accused has made his point.'

But it wasn't over as easily as that.

After a hurried conference, Kinane's lawyer told the court that every man who had been with Jesse that day they had confronted the West Texans and their herd of mavericks, was prepared to swear Drew had meant to kill Jesse, but he was lucky his horse had moved just as Drew fired. The same men contended that no matter what Drew just proved out in the courtyard, he *had* had his gun out of leather at the time, whipped it up and fired even before Jesse could trigger his warning shot.

'Which was all I was intendin', Judge,' Kinane added, turning to gesture towards a young man sitting a couple of rows back, holding hands with Judge Lacy's youngest daughter. 'Your future son-in-law was there, Judge. He'll back me, I'm sure.'

The Cameron boy flushed deeply when all attention focused on him, and the girl nudged him until he stood up, coughed a couple of times and said in a shaky voice,

'Well, I guess that's right, Judge — I mean, I saw what Drew did out back there, but — well, things weren't the same. He was riled out in Pinchnose Pass and I reckon — '

The judge signalled the boy to stop right there and after some deliberation with the settlers' lawyer Lacy delivered his verdict:

'I'm satisfied Drew Hardy is probably the fastest gun in Hangtree County. From what I know of him, he's fairly

39

even-tempered, but he's always been strongly protective of family, and if he was riled, as these gentlemen all swear to, I am ready to agree he would be prepared to kill in order to protect Emmett.'

'I didn't shoot to kill, Judge! Not at Jesse!'

'Quiet, boy, or it'll go ill with you!'

'You mean it ain't so far?'

Pausing and glaring at Drew's bitter tone, Lacy pronounced, 'I find you guilty of attempted murder and the grievous wounding of Jesse Kinane. You are hereby sentenced to seven years in the Hudspeth Penitentiary, starting this day. As for killing Quitar, I am prepared to consider it as an act of self-defence.'

* * *

So Drew Hardy commenced his sentence of seven years in Hell, which he figured was a much more appropriate name for Hudspeth, that very afternoon.

40

Emmett tackled the lawyer, Case Chambers, he had hired and the man looked uncomfortable as he made his excuses for not getting Drew off: he contended it would do his career no good at all if he challenged the judge's verdict.

'Hell, Emmett, Lacy's on his way to the State Senate. He'll remember his friends and enemies — and those who rocked the boat and who didn't.'

'You're fired, you soft-bellied son of a bitch! No one in the Hardy family will ever hire you again.'

That was four years before, Drew recollected, as the big stage rocked along the narrow, rutted trail.

Four years — two appeals against the findings thrown out of court — and he had only seen Emmett twice in all that time, hadn't known about his fall from his horse, or his failing heart, never even knew why the old man stopped visiting and never wrote.

But seeing the smug faces of Kerry and Luke at that Boot Hill graveside, listening to their advice to him never to come back to Lazy H — he knew something had happened while he had been locked-up, something that had turned Emmett against him, so his father was willing to let him rot in Hudspeth . . .

Just how he was ever going to find out what it was he didn't know, but it would have to wait till the end of the three years he had yet to serve. There was no chance they would be pared down. OK! He would serve out his time, and to hell with them all . . .

Then he would find out — he might have to practise mighty hard to recover the speed of his fast draw, unable to do so in prison, but he would do it, all right . . .

'Whatever it takes!' he murmured, causing Hume to stir slightly where the big guard dozed with his head resting against Drew's right shoulder. 'Whatever — and for however long.'

When he glanced up he was startled to see that young girl with the shoulder-length chestnut hair, the one who had giggled earlier, watching him with a warm, soft look on her slightly freckled face. She jumped a little when she realized he had caught her observing him, ducked her head swiftly, but peeked out with one eye between spread fingers and gave him a half-smile . . .

It did little to ease the knowledge he was going to be stuck behind stone walls with a fourteen-pound sledgehammer in his hands for another three years.

But he was wrong about that.

* * *

The big stage coach overturned at the second ford, the one where it had bogged-down on the way to Hangtree for Emmett Hardy's funeral.

There had been rain somewhere up in the hills and the flood waters had surged down between times, scouring the bottom, bringing down more rocks and rubbish, including waterlogged tree trunks. The driver was foolish to try to cross without first stopping to examine the river crossing. It was obvious the rushing waters were going to be halfway up the big wheels, submerging the axles. But Flank Ashby had a hangover and was suffering blinding headaches that slowed his thinking. He saw the muddy, foaming flood all right, but by the time it seeped through the remaining alcohol fumes the team had plunged straight in as usual.

The creek bottom had changed — drastically. It was littered with melon-sized rocks and splintered branches and two large tree trunks. The branches of one protruded above the surface and the team instinctively dodged this — but stepped clear off the ford, the edges having broken away. They plunged and snorted and reared and thrashed.

The twisting and jerking dragged the stage's left-hand wheels off the crumbling edge of the ford and even an Abbott-Downing built stage coach could not defy the forces of gravity. The big vehicle crashed on to its side, woodwork splintering.

Flank Ashby was hurled sixteen feet, four of them up into a sagging tree where he wedged amongst the lower branches. There was no guard on this regular passenger run, so that only left the passengers.

The screams of the women and girls were quickly drowned by the surging flood. One door crumbled, jammed half open, taking the weight of the coach for a short time. Bodies tumbled out, the two gentlemen first, only one of whom paused to plunge back in and grab the thrashing panic-stricken girls and the women. Or he tried. He got hold of one of the girls and literally threw her from him, reaching for anyone else he could find. Then the thrashing, whinnying team broke free, causing the supporting door to crumple. The stage crashed down, pinning the man by one leg. He screamed in pain.

Drew Hardy and his two guards had

been in the seat against the rear wall. It had bulged in with the weight of luggage in the boot behind it when the stage rolled. Hume was pinned against the wooden wall, blood from his busted nose filling his throat as well as the muddy water, slowly drowning him. Grissom was thrown forward, jammed at an odd angle, head downwards.

Drew somehow fared best. He had been squeezed out by the two bodies of his guards and flung over the sagging back of the seat in front. He found himself twisting like a mad corkscrew in a surge that hurled him upwards so that he crashed against the door that was above his head, on the upper side of the coach that was still a few inches above the roaring water. Half blinded, ribs aching from some unremembered blow, he glimpsed a blur of colour and reached out with his cuffed hands, numbed fingers groping.

Acting by pure instinct, he kicked out, felt his boots touch something solid and bent his knees to propel himself up, dragging the burden he had clawed into, smashing the already splintered door. On the surface his ears filled with the roaring of unstoppable flood that smashed into his face and shoulders, tumbling him. Somehow he managed to thrust the young freckled-faced girl whose clothes he had grabbed, up into the air, straining, the manacles biting deeply into his wrists, blood running down his arms. She coughed and screamed and vomited as he waded to the bank and unceremoniously threw her on to the torn grass.

Without even realizing what he was doing, still manacled, he dived back down, struck his head and knees on the coach as it scraped over the rocks, groped inside and tangled in a leather belt. He heaved, boots braced against the now splintering woodwork, and half-dragged Grissom out, scraping the man's face badly on the splintered door. Blood clouded the water but he managed to stand on the coach side and roll Grissom off into shallows where he jammed between the stage and the muddy bank, bloody-face turned towards the sun.

The next groping dive brought up the man whose leg had been jammed: splintering woodwork allowed him to haul the man free. Blinking water from his stinging eyes, Drew saw that everyone was out now, the girls and women hugging each other, sobbing or retching, the men sprawled — everyone except for Hume.

He hesitated, then dragged down one more painful breath and plunged beneath the rushing surface . . .

'By God!' gasped the father of the girls who were clinging to him now, crying and shuddering. 'That man's a true hero!'

4

Crusader

'The thing is, the man, Hume, had ill-treated Drew Hardy all along, yet, still wearing his manacles, Hardy not only rescued my family and me, but he went back and brought out Hume — when he could have very well have left the man to drown after the way he had tormented him! Now I want that story printed within a frame and bold type, smack in the middle of the front page of the *El Paso Courier* — Special edition.'

Cam Foley crossed his office in the front of the *Courier* building awkwardly because he wasn't used to a crutch, but his damaged leg required this extra support right now. He stood at the window, looking out on to El Paso's Plaza del Sol.

'I was never pleased at Judge Lacy's decision at the trial of that Hardy boy, four years ago, but I didn't own majority shares in this newspaper then. I was impressed by the way he protected his father, without hesitation — and, of course, they turned that against him, made it look like he acted almost with premeditation. Well, now I've seen Drew Hardy in action, I'm going to push this all the way to Congress if I have to!' He turned back to look at the haggard man sitting in a chair by one end of the large desk with his legs crossed, ink-stained fingers holding a pencil poised above a dog-eared notebook.

'Well, Casey? What is it you want to say? I can see you're about to burst.'

'Chief, I've worked for you for a long time an' I've seen you go on crusades that would make the Devil himself back-off. Some were good — you forced that under-the-counter railroad deal into the open, got the nesters better treatment — but this time you're going up against a State Senator. Lacy isn't Judge Lacy any more — he's Senator Lacy and he's always been mighty touchy — so you criticize him, even for something he did four years ago, he's gonna come down on you like a rockfall in Pinchnose Pass. And that pass is mighty narrow. It just couldn't miss whoever was caught up in it.'

Cam Foley smiled crookedly. 'You've worked for me for a long time as you say, Case. Surely you know by now I'm in my element when I have a tough fight on my hands — I come alive, man! Oh, I love my family and thoroughly enjoy every moment I can spend with them, but — and this is just between you and me — *nothing*, not even my beloved family, can make me feel the way I do when I'm on one of my crusades, as you call them. I am going to get that boy's sentence reduced if I have to contrive an audience with the President himself!'

Casey shook his head slowly. 'I know you mean it, Chief . . . '

'Then, why are you still sitting here?'

Casey Hadden smiled, showing stained, uneven teeth as he heaved to his feet with a grunt. 'On my way, Chief. I'll have the first draft on your desk by sundown.'

'An hour before sundown,' Foley called, leaning on his crutch as he took a cigar case from his jacket pocket and danced on one leg as he juggled a long, fat cigar out. 'And it had better include an interview with Drew Hardy!'

'Judas priest! You expect a man of my age to ride all the way up to Hudspeth and fight Warden O'Halloran even to see Hardy, let alone interview him?'

'I'll work on my editorial and get a headline down to the typesetters, all ready for your copy — one hour before sundown, Casey. Don't waste time, man! *Go!*'

As Casey shuffled out, Foley fired up his cigar and looked at the glowing tip. He was burning with enthusiasm far hotter than the expensive tobacco leaf. 'That boy saved my family and me! He *will* be rewarded!'

Kerry Hardy reined down by the corral where his brother Luke was setting up another panel of posts-and-rails with two cowboys. Swinging out of the saddle, he called to Luke, and when the man looked up, face sweaty and grimy, he jerked a thumb towards the house.

'Now!'

'What? Earlier you were bitchin' because this section of the corral wasn't finished. Well, it won't *be* finished you keep callin' me away!'

'I said *now!*'

Kerry yanked his saddle-bags off his horse and shouted to one of the cowhands to unsaddle the mount and rub it down, turning to storm across the yard, kicking squawking, foraging chickens out of his way.

He was pacing the parlour, an almost empty glass of whiskey in one hand, when Luke came idling in, tugging off his work gloves.

'You son of a bitch! You *move* when I tell you!'

Luke stopped, blinking. 'Well, pardon me all to hell, big brother! I'm equal owner of this place and you don't gimme orders like you do the wrangler or the goddamn cook!'

'I do if I feel like it,' growled Kerry, tossing down the rest of his whiskey. 'Take a look at the paper there on the desk — Jesus Christ! *There!* How many newspapers you see lyin' there?'

'You never said 'newspaper', you only — Aw, hell!' Luke had picked up the copy of the latest edition of the *El Paso Courier*, and he ran a tongue around his lips as he read the blazing headlines:

Hero or Killer?
Reward or Rockpile?
Prisoner Risks Life Saving Families
Casey Hadden Investigates

'That's only the start,' Kerry said bitterly, refilling his glass and pouring one for Luke whose lips were moving as he read Casey Hadden's article.

'Hell! They *interviewed* Drew! I thought we'd paid O'Halloran to see that Drew never even got any mail, let alone an interview by some goddamn reporter!'

'Not just any reporter — this by Casey Hadden! Top man, has his stuff published in nearly every newspaper on both coasts! And it gets worse — Drew rescued Foley and his family when the stage crashed. Now Foley's on one of his goddamn crusades and he wants Drew set free!'

'He can't do that!'

'I'd like to think so. But Cam Foley's a stubborn sonofa once he gets started on somethin' like this an' he dotes on them two girls of his. Drew pulled 'em both out of that stagecoach while still wearin' his handcuffs.'

'Says he even dragged Hume out, after he'd roughed-up Drew at every chance! Aw, hell, Ker, this is bad! But mebbe Foley ain't big enough to talk Judge — I mean *Senator* — Lacy around.'

'You damn fool! He won't stop with Lacy. Foley's mighty powerful, has interests in some of the big newspapers back East. Got plenty of clout. He'll take it as high as he can go. And you know who the other man was he dragged outta that stage wreck? Murrel, part-owner of several newspapers, includin' the *El Paso Courier* — and brother of a US Congressman!'

'The hell were they doin' on that stage?'

'They belong to the same clubs back East and Foley was showin' Murrel the county. And his 'sweet little girls' wanted to see what it was like to ride in a real Western stagecoach instead of in their usual private railroad car!'

He almost spat on the floor, stopped himself just in time. 'Goddamnit, Luke, it's like it was all set-up, just to clobber us!'

Luke had downed his whiskey without even noticing and now grabbed the bottle and filled the glass to the brim. He drank half in one gulp.

'Aw, I don't b'lieve in that fate stuff. Queer, though, gotta admit. But — there's nothin' Foley can really do, is there? I mean, even if he somehow got Drew a pardon?'

'A pardon! Don't even think about that! Getting him even a couple of months off them three years he's still looking at would be bad enough, but a *pardon!* Man, we can kiss Lazy H goodbye if ever that happens!'

Luke swallowed the last of his drink and stared steadily at Kerry, bringing a frown to the older brother's face.

'What the hell you looking like that for?'

'We just gotta see it don't happen, Ker. No, don't wave your hand at me like that — I know it's obvious an' it won't be easy, but it don't make no difference. Foley's gotta be stopped, big brother, *gotta be!*'

⋆　⋆　⋆

Hume walked up behind Drew Hardy as the man raised the sledgehammer, set himself, and swung a wide kick into the back of Hardy's thigh. The muscle knotted and the leg collapsed. As Drew fell the heavy sledgehammer dropped and he instinctively jerked his head aside. The battered, chipped fourteen-pound hammerhead missed him by an inch.

Gasping, he rolled on to this side, saw Hume standing there, hands on hips, teeth bared. 'Shoot! Thought you might get a busted skull outta that!'

Drew said nothing, but slowly and awkwardly clambered to his feet, his ankles confined by the two feet of chain and leg irons, thigh thundering with new pain. He wasn't surprised by Hume's kick: the man had treated him more roughly than ever since they had returned from the funeral. But thanks to Foley's *El Paso Courier* labelling him a hero and giving a vivid description of his rescue of the stagecoach passengers — including Hume himself — he had gotten a little more respect from most prison guards. But Hume had treated him worse than ever, as if he actually resented Drew having rescued him. If it had been someone else, maybe he wouldn't have felt so bad about it, but Drew Hardy, of all people!

'For about the thousandth time, Hume, I wish like hell I'd left you to drown.'

'Well, you didn't, and you're gonna remember me till the day you die.' Hume reached out, grabbed him by the shoulder and shoved roughly so that Drew staggered, but just managed to keep his footing with the ankle chain catching on some of the granite rock he had been smashing up.

'Warden wants to see you, so hurry it up.'

The words stopped Drew dead: the warden never wanted to see anybody unless it meant trouble — and he was trying desperately to recall if he had done anything wrong lately that could be classed as bad enough for him to be dragged up in front of Warden O'Halloran.

There had been nothing out of the

ordinary — the usual fights and bullying, the animal greed at chow time, the schoolboy challenges of troublemakers demanding he move from their part of the long form he was sitting on — just the usual in-prison hassles, mostly ignored by the guards.

Then he staggered and did fall this time, taken off guard. Hume smiled crookedly, shaking the big hand he had just used to slap the prisoner across the side of the head.

He swung a kick into Drew's side. 'Get up and *run* to the warden's office — and I wanta see them knees right up under your chin while you're doin' it!'

Then he spun quickly as someone approached.

'Don't you ever let up?' demanded Grissom as he limped up, one foot still swollen and bruised from the long-ago stage wreck: permanent damage, but he was grateful to be alive.

Hume grinned. 'Why should I? I hate the bastard and always will. He might leave here at the end of his sentence, but he'll carry memories of Hudspeth to his grave, I'll see to that.' He kicked Drew's leg again and the man staggered, but Grissom grabbed his flailing arm before he lost complete balance, steadying him.

'I hope I run into you on the outside, Hume,' panted Drew. 'Mebbe I'll even come looking for you.'

Hume's face tightened and one hand balled into a fist but Grissom, still gripping Hardy's arm, got between them, and started towards the administration building where the warden had his office on the first floor, pulling Drew with him.

'Warden sent me down to hurry things along,' Grissom said with a tight grin to Hume. 'You holdin' everyone up.'

Hume paled. 'He-he's been — watchin'?'

'Not just him. He's got visitors. Mighty important visitors. They were all at the warden's big window when he sent me down to bring Drew up. I was you, Hume, I'd find something to do on the other side of the quarry, out of sight of the warden's office. And *stay* there

61

till sundown.' Hume swallowed as Grissom guided the stumbling Hardy towards the big greystone building.

When they reached Warden O'Halloran's office, the wizened little man with the close-set and notoriously bad eyes, like a snake's, stepped briefly outside, half-closing the door behind him. He spoke in a hissing whisper, something flickering in the deep black depths of those mean eyes.

'Jesus Christ, what's wrong with that fool, Hume! Putting on a show like that with those men inside watching!' Spittle flew as he jerked a thumb back over his shoulder. Grissom didn't answer — couldn't think of anything to say that O'Halloran would like to hear. 'Get Hume, set him down in the storeroom and tell him not to move. I'll be down to see him soon's I'm finished here.'

Grissom nodded, winked at Drew Hardy and then hurried away. Drew stiffened as the warden took his arm, fingers digging in like steel hooks, and opened the office door.

'Come on in, Drew,' he said in a quiet, friendly tone Hardy had never heard in all his time here at Hudspeth. 'I think you should recognize these gentlemen — '

The ankle chain dragged and clunked. Hardy stopped, frowning, then the faces slipped into his memory: the two men who had been travelling on the stage coach after leaving Hangtree. Foley, a newspaperman of some sort, and the other — he didn't remember hearing his name, but one of the women had asked after Murrel's Congressman brothers . . .

God almighty! he thought. Now what? Were they going to try him again, maybe hang him after all . . . ?

'Can we have a chair for Mr Hardy, Warden?' Foley asked in clipped tones. 'And let's get rid of that leg chain, eh?'

Drew couldn't believe his eyes when O'Halloran bustled about like a hotel porter looking forward to a big tip, found a key and, hands fumbling, unlocked his leg chains.

'That's better,' Foley said as he and his companion smiled. 'Now, I think we could all benefit from a snifter of that whiskey I see in your decanter there, Warden. Then we'll get down to business. All right?'

5

Lonely Lands

As he worked the dappled-grey gelding down the narrow, descending trail, Drew Hardy still couldn't believe that he was a free man for the first time in almost five years. Over a year cut off his sentence!

He shook his head for maybe the hundredth time since riding through the gates of Hudspeth Penitentiary, half-expecting one of the wall guards to put a bullet in his back. He simply could not believe Cam Foley and his companion, Brent Overmeyer (inventor of the world-famous in-home sewing machine of that name) had negotiated — no! had told O'Halloran that Drew was to be set free in three days' time. He was to be outfitted for the trail, including mount and firearms — unloaded: he could load after clearing Hudspeth's boundaries. That should keep everybody happy . . .

Then they had produced the legal papers to back up their demands.

O'Halloran had looked as if he would like to disappear into a crack in the floor, and kept wetting his lips with his tongue. His voice was even raspier than usual, but maybe that was caused by his suddenly dry throat.

'I-I wasn't consulted on this.'

'Nor were you meant to be, nor will be,' Overmeyer said, spreading out a handful of papers on the warden's desk, like a hand of cards. Dead Man's Hand, maybe. 'All in order, under the Seal of Congress, as you will note.'

O'Halloran swallowed, tried to recover, narrowing his mean eyes as he looked at the silent, stunned, Hardy.

'Don't he need another trial?'

'Just read the papers,' said Foley curtly. 'If you have even a faint understanding of legalese, they will tell you about mistrials and presiding judges who exceed their authority. We've taken a lot of trouble and a lot of time preparing these, under congressional advisement, Warden. There are no loopholes. You are to do exactly as they instruct you.' He turned his gaze to Drew, speaking more politely, then, 'Of course, that rescue at the river ford did your case no harm, Mr Hardy. No harm at all.'

Drew cleared his throat. 'Well I never thought about anything like this. Not that I'm complaining, mind!'

Foley and Overmeyer both smiled. 'Of course not. But you should be rewarded, and you shall be. We think a man's freedom is about the best reward anyone could ask for.'

Hardy suddenly grinned. 'I'll go along with you on that, sir!'

⋆   ⋆   ⋆

It was a mad whirl after that. There seemed to be men in frock coats with sagging valises appearing from everywhere, day after day. O'Halloran was stood-down, awaiting investigation into his running of the prison — and his more-than-healthy bank account. Hume and several other guards were fired on the spot, warned that prosecution might well still await them for many breaches of the Prison Wardens' Code,

Doctors whom Drew had never seen before came and examined him, probed and poked his hard-muscled but half-starved frame, procured decent boots to help support the injured instep Hume had given him, even fixed some decay in two molars due to the lousy prison food. Drew hadn't enjoyed *that* time with the dentist, but was grateful after the ordeal was over just the same: those teeth had been paining him for weeks.

Then had come new clothes, second-hand but clean enough and still durable, followed by the return of his six-gun, empty, in its rig, and his saddle. The leather had dried and cracked due to long neglect in Hudspeth's gloomy store-room, but that could be fixed with a little neatsfoot oil and some elbow grease.

His rifle could not be found. Someone had no doubt taken a liking to that particular long-barrelled Henry firearm that Emmett had had made specially for him on his sixteenth birthday. But Foley had a well-cared-for Winchester '73, calibre .44, and one of the first lever-action rifles to use centre-fire ammunition. It was a sought-after fire arm, based on the last Model Henry '66, adapted with the addition of a stronger extractor and new magazine with the side-gate loading, destined to become a famous and much sought-after weapon with the brass sideplates. Known as the Yellow Boy, it became Winchester '73, the latest development on the '66 model and didn't change significantly in the next seven years. He was not only free, but loaded for bear!

Grissom had been the only one to wave him off as he rode through the gates. As they shook hands, the guard said, 'I'm only here thanks to you, Drew. Good luck. Hope you can pick up your life where you left off.'

So did Drew — but he figured that might be expecting a mite too much.

★   ★   ★

It was a long winding trail back to Hangtree and Drew made it even longer by following wild paths through lonely stands of timber and mountains that had never known the ring of a settler's axe or smelled the smoke of a pioneer camp oven.

This was his idea of freedom — ride the lonely trails under a blue and cloudless sky, breathe the untainted air, start at the rustle in the bushes that might be an Indian or a wild beast, likely more curious than hostile. Sweetwater streams flowed in several places and while drinking at one he saw three Indians, watching from a butte, making no attempt to hide, letting him know they regarded this as their land, still unsullied by the white man and his destructive ways.

Hiding himself, he watched in mild

amusement after leaving one camp, and two of the Indians came slinking in, wary as hell as was their way, understandably so, as they checked what spoor he might have left behind.

There was little to show anyone had been there and he saw the surprise on their painted faces: here was someone, a *white* man, who had left little more than a faint footprint to show he had visited this place. Ride far and well, white man.

And then he realized what he was doing: he was deliberately delaying his return to Lazy H. No one had visited or written him since long before Emmett's funeral. In fact, he had had no mail for years and this was one of the things O'Halloran was to be questioned about. He had no notion of what was happening at the ranch, what his brothers were doing, how Emmett had set out his will, what sort of reception he could expect. But no use putting it off . . .

So, no more delays: it was straight

home to the Lazy H, now: leastways, he hoped it would still be 'home'.

*　　*　　*

But the rest of his journey was destined not to be as pleasant as this first part had been.

Riding through a sandy canyon, clear of the lonely lands and on the regular trail from Hudspeth to Hangtree, someone was waiting for him: with a rifle.

The glare from the canyon floor beat up under the brim of his hat and caused him to squint, although he already had been doing so a little, because of the wind moaning through, lifting a thin mist of sand to blur his vision.

There was a brief patch of light up on a ledge about ten feet below the crest of a rocky spur. Without the blurring sand-mist he would have identified it instantly as the flash of sunlight along the barrel of a lifted rifle.

There was a brief delay while his brain sorted this out — only a brief second or two — but sufficient to keep him in the saddle just a mite too long.

As he felt the impact of the bullet striking his chest between his left arm and his upper ribs, he heard the blast of the gun. By then he was toppling over the horse's rump and the old instincts had him snatching at the rifle butt in the saddle scabbard: no cowboy liked to be parted from his horse without a rifle far from the ranch house.

He was lucky: his hand closed over the stock of the Winchester Foley had given him and his falling weight broke the rawhide tie-thongs, freeing the scabbard. He hit hard, and there was a brief red blur and an explosion of lights like fireworks on the Fourth. Then he bounced, breath driving out of him.

Once again instinct took over and he kept rolling, in towards a low line of rocks. He saw a spurt of sand between him and those rocks, then chips flying from the shale and sand stung his face

73

as the dappled-grey ran off. The rifleman, in his eagerness to nail his target, stood up from behind his sheltering rock as Drew spun in against the ribbon of shale. His side hurt. He could feel a film of warm blood between his body and his inner arm. The fingers of the left hand were maybe a mite stiffer than usual, but he managed to work the lever of the unfamiliar rifle.

There was a satisfying, smooth *click* and a shell jacked into the breech. He settled his lean body as the killer raked the shale with the last four shots in his magazine.

Then the man must have realized he made a good target himself and dropped swiftly, just as Hardy fired.

With the heavy hexagonal barrel and the comparative light load of black-powder, there was negligible recoil, so the bullet travelled in an almost flat trajectory, despite being aimed high. His lead ricocheted, but the man's hat spun off and bounced down the slope.

It came to rest upside down at the base of the spur. By then the killer had reloaded — not time for a full magazine, but likely six or seven shells in the tube. He blasted four along the low line of shale in a swift volley that told Drew the man knew what he was doing, could handle a gun better than most ordinary cowboys. Maybe he wasn't an 'ordinary' cowpoke . . .

He didn't like where that thought was taking him, so thrust it out of his mind, concentrated on the movements up there. The dry-gulcher was careless now, maybe shaken up that he hadn't managed to nail Hardy right off, like he should have, given the surprise, the position, and the way he handled his rifle. *Out of practice, maybe . . . . Or nervous . . .*

He was wearing a brown shirt, a darker shade than the rocks where he had set up. Drew glimpsed it passing between two boulders but was unable to see him well enough to identify him. He jerked off his neckerchief and wadded it under his shirt to cover the wound. Seemed to him like the bullet had gone clear through without touching bone or any thing seriously incapacitating: but he had better put his arm to good use before it started to stiffen.

He flung the rifle suddenly to his shoulder, another instinctive reaction, as he glimpsed that moving patch of dark brown again. He worked the lever — *Jeez, it was smooth!* — in two fast cyclings, getting off both shots fast enough for one to spurt rock chips even as the first struck home.

He was sure it was a hit and thought he heard a half-yell of pain. Then the other rifle clattered down from where the man had been knocked off his feet. Well, he wouldn't stick around now he had lost his rifle, Drew figured, shucking two shells from his bullet loops and thumbing them through the spring-loaded gate in the brass side-plates. He writhed around, trying to see how badly the man over there was hit, but felt the first pain from his own wound as the numbness began to wear off. He fell and clung to a rock, getting his breath, straining to see through a redness that curtained briefly behind his eyes.

The dizziness lasted long enough for him to miss the man's movements up there and he swore, holding the rifle in both hands, willing his vision to clear as he watched the general area.

He was way too slow: by the time his vision cleared up, the wounded killer was galloping away through a narrow, twisting passage that took him up and over the spur: he obviously knew the area better than his target did.

Drew swore, eased back against a rock as the grey trotted up to within a few feet, looking curious. At least he would be able to get to his canteen and clean up the wound, slake his thirst and — then what?

With a sudden, unbidden burst of determination, he decided he was going after the killer.

The man must have some good reason for drygulching him — and Drew damn well aimed to find out what it was.

After bandaging the wound as well as he could — the bleeding was slowing now — and swallowing a few deep mouthfuls of water, he led the horse across to where the killer had holed-up, found empty cartridge cases and some smears of blood, as well as a dozen cigarette butts: so the man had been waiting for him for some time . . . The man's battered hat still lay in the hot sun. Drew winced as he leaned down to pick it up, using his left hand, right gripping a boulder's coarse surface.

There was nothing distinctive about the hat — you could see a hundred just like it on the main drag of any large cattle town. He pulled down the sweatband — sometimes a man made his mark underneath the narrow strip of thin leather.

Someone had in this case. *Drago* had

been burned on to the inside of the leather strip with a hot wire.

The only Drago he knew was — or had been — the hardcase ramrod of Lazy H.

6

Going Home

Drew Hardy remembered the man well enough. He had come to Lazy H a year or so before the trouble with the nesters in Pinchnose Pass. He was a tall, lean man, typical Westerner, a drifter who claimed to handle a gun as well or better than he handled horses and cattle — and he reckoned he was a top hand at those things.

He proved it, too, when he entered a turkey shoot to celebrate Hangtree's Anniversary Day by taking out the two top prizes: the birds were shot at extreme ranges and prompted the organizers to pass round the hat and give Drago a cash appreciation of his talents.

He appreciated it all right, and that should have given the town some warning about the kind of man he really was.

As Drew remembered it, Drago celebrated his win, and spent five days in jail afterwards because of damage he had caused to two saloons and a cat-house, as well as injuries inflicted on a couple of men he had beaten-up during the wild night.

It didn't please Emmett, who was all for firing him, but Kerry insisted that Drago was a top hand and the wild wingding was an odd one out: normally, Drago was peaceful and sober enough to get his chores done, and done well at that.

Emmett Hardy still hesitated and Kerry confessed he had known Drago in the army during the War. Both had been Field Medics and Drago had carried a wounded Kerry on his back through enemy lines and the thick of battle to an Aid Post, despite sustaining a head wound himself while doing it.

So Kerry owed the man. 'Saved my life, Pa. He spent longer in hospital recoverin' from his head wound than I did with mine. I told him if ever he needed a hand-out or work, he should look me up.'

Emmett didn't see how he could do anything else but keep Drago on under those circumstances. But the man turned out to be as good as he claimed and was soon *segundo* — and not long afterward, when their ramrod was killed by a maverick's horns, and at Kerry's insistent suggestion, Emmett made Drago foreman of Lazy H.

He didn't regret it: Drago worked the ranch well but was a hard taskmaster and they lost a few good hands because of it: men who weren't about to stand still to have their teeth loosened or their ribs bent when Drago was displeased with their work.

At that time, West Texas was full of no-account drifters and outlaws, so Emmett was reluctant to let Drago go: but he did need a tough ramrod on Lazy H. So he warned Drago not to be so blamed hard on the men or he *would* be fired, regardless. Drago appeared to take it well enough, admitted that he suffered mighty bad headaches at times and that afterwards he didn't always recollect clearly what he had done or who he had hurt — or even why.

But there had been a look on his wolf-lean face — a tightening of the thin lips, slitting of the steely eyes that never held much warmth anyway — when he said it, and Drew remembered that look and the uneasiness he had felt.

'He's a mean one, Pa,' he had opined and Emmett merely nodded, as if he had only half-heard, frowning as he watched Drago stride away with that confident, near arrogant way he had.

'Yeah — well, he saved Kerry's life and so I owe him. Seems Luke didn't know him before he showed up here, but then Luke was an artillery man . . . '

Drew hadn't thought about Drago in years, but he recalled there had been quite a ruckus when the man had shot and killed three men in a Hangtree saloon after accusing them of rustling

Lazy H stock. The irate sheriff had investigated and reluctantly had to admit that the evidence was there — the men were guilty.

'And now they're dead!' growled Sheriff Jackson McLane, a middle-sized, fearless man in his forties. He had a sallow colour and a cough that shook him from time to time.

It caught him now and, after half a dozen gasping explosions, he wiped his mouth with his kerchief and said, still annoyed, 'It's *my* job to bring men like that to justice, Drago.'

'Well, I done your job for you. They'd've cleared the county before you were satisfied with your evidence. You oughta be thankin' me, instead of roastin' my butt.'

'You got an attitude I don't care for, Drago. Mebbe you better spend a little time in my jail until you cool down.'

Drago smiled crookedly. 'Now you wouldn't really try to take me in, would you, Sheriff? I mean, I done every rancher in this here county a *favour*!

And you wanta lock me up? Hey, you remember this is election year . . . ?'

Many in the watching crowd nodded, and some murmured open support for Drago. These were mostly ranchers and settlers from out on the range: the townsmen tended to back the sheriff.

But McLane had recently been told by the local sawbones that there was a good chance he would develop tuberculosis within six months. So McLane backed-off — he had a wife, two daughters and an ailing mother to support: keeping his pension was more important than winning a victory over this loudmouthed son of a bitch that counted for little.

It surprised the town though, his backing-down — McLane had persuaded the doctor to keep the news about his lung fever quiet, though he told a few of his closest friends. One was Emmett Hardy, and he defended the sheriff's action — or lack of action — when Drew brought home the story from town.

'Jackson McLane's a good man and a hard-workin' sheriff. He'd have his own reasons for backin' down and none of 'em would be because he lacked guts. You know, he gave this town its name? Used to be called Cottonwood — some-one must've strained his brain to think up that name, seein' as we have that one giant cottonwood in the middle of Main. You were only a shaver then . . . '

That was true, but Drew remembered just the same: a bunch of hardcases hit town and McLane had them picked for trouble right off. But one of them got behind him and laid him out and they locked him in his own cells, shot his deputy — then cut loose.

They shot up the place and one of the stray bullets cut down and killed a girl child — and that was that as far as the till-then cowed citizens were con-cerned.

They turned into a mob three seconds after the doctor pronounced the little girl dead. Some of them were shot, one townsman later dying of his wounds, but the rest overwhelmed the hardcases and lynched the four who survived — strung them up on that lone cottonwood which had a long, almost horizontal freak of a branch projecting from the north side. It was at a perfect height to swing a man from and give him room to kick and twitch and convulse at the end of a rope . . .

By then McLane's yells had been heard and someone let him out. He actually shot and wounded two townsmen before they calmed down and stepped back before his lashing tongue: basically, he told them, in scathing language, he simply could not *believe* the law-abiding citizens of Cottonwood could behave in this way! *A damn, rabid lynch mob! Animals*!

They would be the shame of West Texas — 'Damn well ought to call the place 'Hangtree' so you'll be reminded for the rest of your lives of what you've done!'

The citizens were a decent lot and, fact was, many of them were kind of queasy and shaky after realizing how they had allowed this thing to happen. But no one, not even Jackson McLane, was sorry those hardcases had swung for their foul deeds . . .

The town didn't need the 'Hangtree' tag to remember, but the name stuck and it appeared as such on the next Ordnance Survey Map, so that made it official. *Hangtree, West Texas.*

But the lynched men had swung and turned in the wind all that night — no one had the energy, or desire, to cut them down — but just before full sunup, someone shot the ropes through and the bodies crashed to the dust. A lone rider quit town right after. He was never identified, but when Drago turned up sometime later to join the Lazy H, the saloon swamper who had seen that rider leaving Hangtree, figured Drago looked a helluva lot like the man most suspected of the deed. Not that it really mattered.

No one ever proved it, never even tried, as far as Drew knew.

But whoever had done it had been a marksman — the empty cartridge cases had been found seventy yards away on the roof of the feed barn downstreet from the cottonwood. And Drago had proved he was a mighty fine rifle shot in that turkey shoot.

So that was how Drew Hardy remembered Drago.

Now, feeling somewhat feverish from his wound, which was hot and growing stiffer, Drew tossed the old hat aside, deciding he could accept that Drago was the man who had bushwhacked him.

But *why* . . . ?

He had never crossed swords with him on Lazy H or anywhere else. He didn't like the man and his bullying, arrogant ways, but they had been civil enough to each other and only came into contact during working hours, anyway.

So the question still remained: why would Drago — or anyone else for that matter — want to kill him so soon after his release from Hudspeth Penitentiary?

The only way to find out was to track down the would-be killer and hope the sonofa wasn't fit enough to lie-up some place and wait for him to show so he could put a bullet in his back.

And really finish the job.

* * *

Drago tried.

But he only had his six-gun now and, though he was probably a pretty good shot with the Colt, it wasn't the same as a rifle.

Drew Hardy was feeling poorly as he rode his dappled-grey into a series of clustered hillocks — too small to be called hills, too large to be termed simply rises. It was nearing the end of the day, sun heeled over, drawing long-fingered shadows, moving them slowly as the disc sank lower, as if pointing him out to the waiting ambusher.

The wound under his arm had

stiffened most of that side and he was sure he could hear his shoulder bones creak when he moved. He had a headache and the glare hurt his eyes, and his thirst was so great he only recalled ever experiencing its intensity once before, maybe twice, if he counted a long, long session on the Hudspeth rockpile. The other time was when his horse had been killed by a rattler and had slid over a ledge, taking his canteen and saddle gear with it — and the waterless alkali that stood between him and an Indian well he knew of stretched away to the horizon . . .

Thirst would take a man's mind and twist it up and wring it out like nothing else would — not even hunger. He was past sweating and his flesh was hot to touch. He reeled slightly in the saddle — and the unplanned movement saved his life.

A six-gun boomed from ahead and above, three times, two fast shots, followed by a slight pause and then the third. The bullets tore past him like bees with their tails afire — and if he hadn't swayed the way he had, at that exact angle, he would have been a dead man.

As it was, instinct took over once more and he allowed himself to fall sideways, hit the patch of sand he had noticed wind-built into a small hummock, and scrabbled his way in behind it. He knocked off his hat so that it hung down his back by the rawhide chinstrap, and brought up his Colt. It was his own, but had not had any care in the Hudspeth storeroom and he hadn't yet had time, tools nor oil to give it the attention it needed.

The hammer was stiff and the bushwhacker — it had to be Drago — got off his fourth and fifth shots. Then the gun went silent — which meant he had only loaded five shells, keeping an empty chamber for under the hammer while travelling — or he had a sixth shot, and was saving it for when Drew made a move, showing himself . . .

He would wait a long time. Drew had been taught this kind of patience by Emmett long ago when they had cornered a bunch of horse thieves in a dead-end canyon: they had waited and sweated, without water or shelter, for nine hours before the thieves decided they had had enough and made their run — which ended abruptly for all five outlaws.

Now the sun, though westering, hammered his already burning flesh. His mouth was dry but he couldn't reach the nearly empty canteen on the grey without revealing his position. The mount pawed the ground and moved to get in the scant shade.

Hell, *no*! Drew yelled inside his head, and winced as Drago fired at the now exposed animal.

But the man missed and that told Drew what kind of shape Drago was in. Then he saw that dark brown shirt against the reddish hue of the hillock that hid the killer. He fired, surprised at how much effort it took to pull the unoiled trigger. The Colt jumped in his grip and he threw down again, certain he had missed with the first shot, got off a second. When the gunsmoke cleared he saw Drago was down, face down, sprawled over the low ridge that had hidden him.

He couldn't see the man's right hand the way he was lying, and Drew slid down from his own position, watching Drago every moment, as he reached for the horse, then the scabbard, and freed the Winchester.

He levered in a shell — much smoother than the Colt's mechanism — and, half-crouched, gritting his teeth against the pain it caused him, he circled around until he was slightly above Drago and could see his right hand.

It still held his Colt. And then Drago lifted and rolled on to his side, the six-gun coming up fast, but wobbly.

He never got off that sixth shot he had been saving.

Drew Hardy's bullet smashed into

the man's arm just above the elbow and Drago yelled in blazing pain as his jerking limb flung outwards, gun dropping, wrenching his body around on to his back.

He was lying there, left arm across his torso, hugging the shattered, bloody arm, gritting his teeth against dreadful pain, as Drew walked up, smoking rifle covering him.

But there was no more fight left in Drago.

7

Drago

So this was Drago — mighty near the end of his line. His face was streaked with blood, hair matted with it on one side. Drew frowned and leaned a little closer — there seemed to be a hollow just to the rear of his right ear that was sticky and red. He moved his gaze and saw more blood on the man's chest and, of course, there was the shattered arm.

It was a wonder Drago was even conscious: there must be tremendous pain.

But the steely eyes glared through the clouding of agony and the mouth moved, the tongue licking involuntarily at the salty blood passing over those thin lips.

'You li'l — bastard. You — you've done for me.'

It was a hoarse, rasping, breathless

gasp — but there was plenty of venom in it.

'You mean — you weren't trying to kill me? Did I miss something? Like this was supposed to some be kinda game?'

The chest heaved and Drew thought he heard a sucking sound, bubbling sound — *likely lung-shot*.

'Huh! Called you — 'little'. You ain't the li'l Drew as I recall. Still lean as a rail but — but lotsa — muscle.'

'You can get some just like it — by swingin' a fourteen-pound sledge and bouncing it off granite and basalt, every goddamn day for more'n five years. 'Course, you work up an appetite, but you never get fed properly. Keeps the weight down, though.'

'Sassy! You was — always — sassy!'

Drew squatted, still holding the rifle. 'Drago, there's nothing I can do for you — except bury you.'

'You — you damn well — *wait!*' There was sudden, raw fear in the man. 'Don't — don't you bury me before I-I croak!'

Drew's eyes narrowed. *The man was terrified at the thought of being buried alive! With reason, sure, but — maybe that could be put to good use . . .*

'Drago, I ain't got a lot of time. I've had all those years in Hudspeth to think about Kerry and Luke running Lazy H. Wondering what happened to Pa. Yeah, yeah, of course I know he's dead, but I'd never heard anything about a fall from a horse or heart problems. He suddenly stopped writing — no visits. I've got a heap of questions and I reckon only Kerry and Luke can answer them. So, you hurry up and die or I'll either ride on and leave you to die alone' — another flare behind those now worried-looking eyes — 'or I'll push you into that crevice and kick a few pounds of dirt on top of you — '

Drago was writhing now, teeth biting into his bottom lip. He made guttural sounds but was so terrified he couldn't form any words.

Drew thumbed back his hat, glanced at the sky, and shook his head slowly as he turned his gaze back to the dying man. 'Reckon I better be going, Drago.'

He stood and Drago coughed a spray of blood, tried feebly to touch Drew's boot with his left hand.

'Wait! I — I can't tell you much . . .'

'Well, tell me what you know, but make it short.'

'Aw — God*damn*! But you — you've turned into a mean one!' Drago gasped and put up a hand to the dent in the side of his head. 'See this? A tin plate they clipped over a hole in my skull durin' the war. Some damn sawbones had been to South America and said the old Inca Indians there used to cut a piece out of a man's skull, replace it with a curve of coconut shell or shaped animal bone. So, the sonofa — did it to me! Cut up a coffee can! I — fell an' hit it when you — nailed me back there. I can feel it — pressin' on my brain. They warned me it could happen and — I'd suffer all kindsa hell before it finished me. I tell you what I know and you — gimme a quick bullet, eh? Through the ticker — between the eyes — any-where it'll finish me — quick.'

Drew was taken aback by the request. He felt uneasy under the intense stare of Drago. His heart beat faster — *he didn't know if he could do it*! Shoot a helpless man, even at that man's request. Then, again, the poor devil was suffering, already half out of his head, and there was no way he could survive. Cutting the agony short would be doing him a favour: but it was still a chore he shied away from.

He kept his face blank, almost indifferent.

'Damn — you! Gimme your — word!'

Drew tightened his lips, abruptly nodded. There! Now he would have to do it. 'All right, Drago — you've got it.'

'Even if I — dunno — much . . . ?'

Drew nodded again. 'Whatever you can tell me.'

Drago seemed to relax a little but abruptly gave a strangled scream that made Drew jump so that he lost balance and sat down. When the wave of pain had passed Drago began to talk. Drew brought his canteen, gave him some water from time to time. There wasn't a lot of detail, more a sketchy outline, but it was more than Drew Hardy knew: he had lived in ignorance of quite a drama while doing his time in Hudspeth, it seemed.

Later, he strung it all together and in some kind of sequence, because Drago's mind wandered and he would jump from one part to another — writhe and yell in agony — spit a couple of words, mutter gibberish, then fall silent.

But it made some kind of sense when Drew pieced it together — after he had buried Drago . . .

★   ★   ★

Emmett Hardy's riding accident had happened when he was alone, scouring the ranges for rounded-up mustangs, due for breaking-in and branding. The wrangler, Mickey Payne, found him with a big wound in his left temple, where he had landed on a rock. He had been tossed over a drop into a dry river bed and busted some ribs and one arm as well.

The horse had to be shot as it had snapped both forelegs. Mickey Payne knew about horses but nothing about injuries: he had simply draped Emmett's unconscious body across his saddle and ridden hell-for-leather back to the ranch.

The sawbones, Doctor Preston Giles, said it had caused a lot more damage to Emmett's brain, not to mention his chest organs — heart, lungs, and the ribs themselves. But the young wrangler had acted quickly and Emmett would probably survive.

He did, but his mind was gone and he was no longer capable of making decisions, so Kerry, being the eldest, took over — with a somewhat wary Luke looking over his shoulder.

They made the decisions and Emmett lingered, gradually deteriorating. He had fluid on the lungs now and the extra pressure put more strain on an already strained heart.

Death was inevitable — only a matter of time. Kerry knew something about medicine from his war service as a field medic so Doc Giles prepared a digitalis solution for Emmett's heart, decongestants for his lungs, salves and lotions for the slow-healing wounds.

Kerry was competent enough, administering these according to Doc Giles's directions, but both he and Luke still worried about the ranch. So they confided in Drago and all three went to see the Lazy H lawyer in Hangtree — Denton 'Denny' Clarke, a man about Kerry's age. He had inherited a run-down law business from his father, who, one of Emmett's contemporaries, had handled Lazy H's affairs almost from its beginnings: old man Clarke was OK, as long as he was sober.

Kerry and Drago knew Clarke from the war. He had been a senior record-keeper in the Medical Corps, with the rank of lieutenant, and had competently handled mountains of correspondence. But he found the task

almost overwhelming once the amaz-
ing, pain-killing drug that had been
derived from morphine and named
after the 'heroes' it was meant to treat,
came into widespread use. They called
it *heroin*.

It was happily fed to the patients on
demand, eliminating the pain of terrible
wounds, before it was realized it was
habit-forming. By then there were
hundreds of wounded soldiers, freed of
pain, but left with a sudden screaming
craving for the drug that could not
easily be satisfied. There were suicides
and savage killings by men driven out of
their heads by the desire for heroin:
there was nothing heroic about the poor
devils caught up in the massive blunder
— administration of the drug without
adequate trial.

The Army introduced all kinds of
regulations for the drug's use — the
Army was good at that kind of thing!
— and, surprisingly enlightened, devised
a strict quota of tapering-off doses for
men affected by it. But it was given only

on official authorization.

And thereby the Army opened up a can of worms.

If a man craving heroin could only get it by an authorized form, then the man in charge of validating such forms was bound to have many offers made to him to slip in an extra authority or two, or a dose outside of a particular schedule.

That was how Denny Clarke made enough money to rescue the ailing legal business left to him by his father, who had died in an alcoholic stupor. Kerry and Drago, on the fringes, learned about this corruption and had used that knowledge to their own advantage on several occasions — Clarke had no redress. They could prove he had forged authorization forms for the drug and had shared in the rake-off when it was later sold at exorbitant rates to those who craved it . . . and would use any means, lawful or not, to get it.

So, after a little reminder of those days when Drago and Kerry went to see Denny Clarke in his Hangtree offices, Clarke soon produced a new will, dated before Emmett's riding accident. This cut Drew out of the original will, where he was meant to inherit a one-third share of Lazy H — because, (so the new will said — in Emmett's surprisingly neat handwriting) *'my youngest son, Drew Emmett Hardy, has disgraced the family name, and, presently serving a sentence in Hudspeth Penitentiary, is hereby disowned by me and is no longer a legatee of this, my last will and testament.'*

It was a perfect forgery: no one could have suspected it hadn't been composed and signed by Emmett himself.

Clarke would have demanded his due, of course, despite the blackmail, but Drago couldn't recall what it was.

Drew, squatting beside the dying man on that hogback rise, felt his head swirling, trying to absorb all the disjointed information Drago had given him.

He felt sick — and then the anger began to simmer in him, rising up, so that he felt a terrible urge to kill his own brothers. That really shook him.

Drago was fading fast, but then slipped into a short lucid period as he lay there, bloody body shuddering with his painful efforts to breathe.

'Drago, right now, this makes no more sense to me than a Chinese gambling ticket, but I can see a thread of something that might mean it's true. I never did like Denny Clarke and I know Emmett had been thinking of switching lawyers . . . I'd sure like to get some proof to back this up.'

Drago rolled his head towards Drew, the lustre beginning to fade from his eyes.

'Ask — her — '

Drew stiffened. 'Who?'

Then, surprisingly, Drago gave a tight, ugly smile. 'If they ain't — already killed her.'

The eyes closed and Drew reached out and shook him by the shoulder. '*Who*, dammit? Who are you talking about?'

But Drago had slipped back, sliding down into the pain that was wrenching him from this world into whatever waited beyond.

He never did regain consciousness: the only relief Drew found in that was that he wouldn't have to steel himself to put a bullet into the man and end his suffering.

It was a hell of a chore burying the man, although Drew picked the softest patch of soil. He couldn't dig too deep — it hurt his wound and set it bleeding again — so he dragged rocks over the small mound, then collapsed, nearly exhausted, mind aswirl . . .

Drago hadn't said Kerry and Luke had sent him to kill Drew but it was certain that's what had happened.

His unexpected release from prison, backed by a congressional order, must have shaken up those two miserable sons of bitches clear down to their run-over boots.

Well — just wait until they met him face to face.

★ ★ ★

The fever was bad that night and he rolled himself up in the thick new blanket he had been given when he had left Hudspeth — the Order of Release had stipulated it be of good quality. He built a fire in a gutter cut by a long-dead stream, screened it as well as he could with deadfalls and huddled close.

Emmett had always taught him that a man could sweat fever out of his system in this way. He had seen it work — partially, anyway — on a cowhand whose foot had been badly mangled by a stomping horse and then had become infected.

The man had shaken the fever but his foot had not survived — it had been amputated by the first doctor they had taken him to. Undeterred, the cowhand had amused himself during his long convalescence by carving himself a wooden foot, even padding it and fitting it into a boot. As far as Drew could remember he was still working the range, up around the Mogollon Rim in Arizona.

He didn't have as much water as he should: it was important to replace the liquid sweated out of the body with fresh water. But when he awoke he was no longer shivering and his aching jaws weren't clamped tight in an effort to keep his teeth from chattering — strange how a man could feel even though he was half-roasted.

He was weak and hungry, gnawed a little jerky, clambered aboard the grey he had left saddled all night and hobbled. He rode slowly away from the area, making his way to the trails that would take him back to Hangtree.

Once he found drinkable water, he stopped to cook the last of his sow-belly and heat his last can of beans. That set him up and he was surprised to realize he hankered strongly after a cigarette. There had been no tobacco ration in prison and he had got to the point where he didn't even miss cigarettes, and hadn't for a couple of years.

But now he felt the craving starting and knew he would be smoking again before long, once he could get his hands on some tobacco and papers.

It happened a couple of hours later when he met two cowhands on their way to Van Horn and they shared their smokes and coffee with him.

He got the conversation around to ranching — he was now past the line of Culberson County and back in Hangtree territory, so he was able to drop in a query about Lazy H.

'Too damn big,' said the cowpoke calling himself Ernie. 'The rannies are livin' in line shacks or campin' out, eating hardtack, hardly ever get to work home pastures — that's for the old hands.'

'Yeah,' his companion agreed, a man named Holt. 'They sure favour them — but they pay pretty well.'

'When you can get it!' Ernie said.

'Tightwads?' Drew asked, still casual.

'Might be. The one called Kerry

seems OK but his brother, Luke, he's kinda miserable. I was you, I'd pass on Lazy H and head south to the Concho spreads. That's where me an' Holt are goin'.'

'Not me. Got some business in Hangtree.'

'Well, if you ain't broke now, you will be after a few days in that place.'

Drew frowned at Ernie. 'How so?'

'Damned expensive, is how so!' Holt allowed. 'They say Lazy H owns the only freight line and they charge what they like. Take it or leave it.'

'Citizens put up with that?'

Ernie shrugged. 'That or go hungry. Besides, the mayor's some kinda lawyer, friendly with Lazy H, them Hardy brothers. Word is they work it between 'em.'

'Didn't they have a tough sheriff — Jackson someone?'

'Think he died — lung fever or somethin'. Law now is said to be bent as a horsehoe.'

Drew said *adios* to the two drifters

and saddled the grey he had turned loose on a patch of lush grass.

Seemed like Hangtree was going to be a lot more interesting than he figured. It sure didn't sound like the place he had known five years before.

But he aimed to find out. If he pushed things a little, he could be there by sundown.

8

Hangtree

Doctor Preston Giles didn't recognize Drew at first as he held up the lantern and let the dull orange glow wash over this tall man standing on his doorstep.

'I was hoping to start my supper, young man. Is yours an urgent problem?'

'Urgent enough, Doc.' Drew held up his bare left arm with the shirt sleeve wrapped around the upper area. The rag was spotted with blood and the flesh looked stretched, tinged pink. 'Not much of a wound, but I think it might be infected.'

Doctor Giles sighed. 'Follow me.'

He led the way down a passage into a shorter hall and opened a narrow door. It was his office, rolltop desk with neatly-stacked piles of papers and cardboard folders, and a few mysterious medical instruments. Giles lit a desk lamp with a green-and-white china shade and turned out the other lantern.

He put on half-moon spectacles to examine Drew's wound and made a small clicking noise with his tongue as he went to a cupboard, brought back a dish and tweezers and a small thin-bladed scalpel.

'Threads from your shirt, no doubt abounding with germs, have been carried in by the bullet. I'll remove them — may have to cut away a little proud flesh — and wash it with eusol.' He placed a hand on Drew's forehead. 'Mmmm — a little fever. Some tincture of willowbark will soon get that down.' He stepped back suddenly, frowning. 'By Godfrey! I know you! Drew Hardy!'

'Long time since you fixed my scraped knees or set my nose, Doc.'

'After a fight with your elder brother, Kerry, as I recall. Er, weren't you — residing — in Hudspeth recently?'

Drew smiled at the doctor's attempt

115

at discretion. 'I was, but I'm a free man, now, Doc, by order of Congress.'

Giles worked as Drew spoke, didn't look up. 'Well, that seems mighty high-falutin', but I'm glad, Drew. Like a lot of other folk, I didn't go along with Judge Lacy being so high-handed and bringing down that sentence.'

'Is he still a senator?'

Giles frowned, glanced up sharply.

Drew shrugged. 'Just wondered.'

'I believe he is still a member of the Senate but not an — active one. There's a rumour he's on notice to resign.' After washing the wound and bandaging it, he gave Drew the bitter willowbark infusion and stepped back. 'That wound would've cleared in a day or so by itself and healed over pretty good. You didn't really need to see me.'

Drew smiled thinly, unrolled the spare shirt he had brought with him from his saddle-bags and put it on, the doctor helping him with that stiff left arm.

'I'm on my way to Denny Clarke. You

being a friend of Emmett's, I figured you might be able to tell me a few things I don't know about his — passing.'

Giles said nothing, went to a small bureau, and brought out a bottle and two shot glasses. He filled both, handed one to Drew. They drank to the memory of Emmett Hardy.

'He — disowned you, boy. You disgraced his name — or it's said that was how he saw things.'

'Someone must've worked mighty hard to convince him of that. Pa knew I'd been railroaded into Hudspeth.'

Giles nodded, refilled both glasses and sipped from his own before speaking again. 'He was not quite — right in the head by that time. You know about his horse throwing him? Yes, I thought so. He was not capable of making a rational decision by himself — but your brothers were on hand to help him, if you know what I'm trying to say, without being too blunt.'

'Be blunt as you like, Doc. I know

what my brothers are capable of.'

'All right — Emmett's mind was affected. His heart was not good. Somehow, with the help of Denton Clarke, they got him to sign a paper giving Kerry and Luke power of attorney. Look, Drew, there's nothing I can prove here and in my position, I daren't go on record with any wild accusations against a man like Denny Clarke.'

Drew tossed down his whiskey but shook his head when the medic offered the bottle again.

'Not used to it, Doc. Never did take to that rotgut they make in Hudspeth from vegetable peelings. Doc, they sent Drago to meet me. That's how come I got this wound.'

'And — Drago?'

'Buried him in the hills, but he did some talking first. Been thinking about what he said as I rode on here. He reckons Kerry and Luke and Clarke forged a new will, cutting me out entirely. I guess it seemed safe enough to do it, with Emmett out of his mind, me in jail and Clarke willing.'

Giles frowned. 'Clarke has always been — suspect — mixed-up in shady dealings. But he has always been astute enough to keep himself in the clear — or to make it look that way. This is dangerous stuff we're talking about here, outright theft. I tend to think Denny would be more — circumspect. As I said, he has always covered himself.'

'And would've this time, too, I reckon. So I figure he's got a copy of the original will somewhere and if Kerry pushes too hard, he can threaten to bring it to light. He'd be in trouble, but Kerry and Luke would have a lot more to lose.'

'You've obviously given this a lot of thought.'

'Haven't had much time, but what Drago told me explained a lot of things. Doc, I'll handle the part about the ranch and any legacy I'm due, but what I really want to know about is Emmett's death.'

The doctor stiffened, poured himself another drink. 'It was heart failure that killed him, Drew. No doubt of it.'

'Uh-huh — but Kerry was the one giving Pa the medicine.' Giles didn't meet his gaze and Drew continued quietly. 'You meet a lot of queer folk in Hudspeth, Doc. One feller worked on the pile with me was doing his time because he poisoned his wife. He was a gardener of some sort, knew about plants and herbs. He admitted to me one day after he'd had a pull or two at that rotgut brew they used to make in the pen, that the first time he tried to poison her, she had survived — but he'd been suspected and jailed. She liked herbal teas, particularly one made from comfrey. He said the digitalis plant is often mistaken for comfrey but a tea made from digitalis is fatal. He'd labelled all his garden plants for her benefit, when the marriage was going well. When it began to sour, he labelled a digitalis plant as comfrey. Right enough, after he was jailed, she had brewed up some tea from it, believing it to be comfrey, and died of a massive heart attack. He was gloating that here he was in prison, but *alive*, while she was dead — and no one suspected that he was responsible.'

Giles turned his glass in his hand slowly. 'An ugly little story. True, I've no doubt, because it's common enough, mistaking digitalis for comfrey.' He took a deep breath. 'All I can say, Drew, is this: I was — uneasy — about Kerry's attitude to Emmett. After I was called when Emmett died, I took back the bottle of digitalis tincture I had given Kerry to administer. I noticed it was more viscous, more syrupy, than it should have been, as if it had been boiled, to concentrate it.'

Drew straightened. 'That'd make it more poisonous?'

'Yes, concentrating the tincture would make it much more poisonous: the normal dose of five drops could well be — lethal . . . That's all I'm prepared to say, Drew. All I *dare* say in my position.'

Drew's face was tight. 'Obliged, Doc. How much?'

'I never sent Emmett a bill in all the years I knew him. I don't aim to break that tradition now, Drew. This town has gone to hell in a hand-basket these last few years, needs pulling up by its bootstraps. If you can help in that respect, help weed out some of the people responsible for its decline — '

Drew Hardy smiled widely. 'Consider it done, Doc.'

Preston knew that was no idle boast.

Then Hardy asked abruptly. 'Lee Dekker.'

Giles raised his eyebrows. 'She took up a sword on your behalf, Drew. I didn't realize you two were that well acquainted.'

'Not so — I knew her slightly at school, but it was mostly because I hung around with her brother, Matt.'

Giles was sober now. 'Always in scrapes. I believe she went to stay with him after she lost her job in town. He had a small spread at the time, somewhere out there in the Diablos. He doesn't have it now, though.'

Drew frowned slightly. 'Lee didn't lose her job because of her hounding O'Halloran to let me come to Emmett's funeral, did she?'

'Perhaps.' Giles looked at him steadily. 'She was Denny Clarke's secretary and book-keeper at the time.'

★ ★ ★

He had noticed a light in Denny Clarke's office on the top floor of a two-storey building called simply, Clarke's. It had been built by his father early on and Denny himself had added the upper floor, keeping it entirely for his law offices. Downstairs he rented to a bootmaker, draper, and freight agent.

The office was reached by a set of narrow, quite steep stairs on the outside of the building, with a small landing and a heavy door at the top. Drew went up easily, using the balls of his feet to save his boots creaking and heels tapping. But he couldn't avoid the loose tread about halfway that made a sudden screech. Was it intentional?

Too late now — if it was meant to give warning, it had fulfilled its purpose.

He was almost at the landing when the heavy door opened and a man carrying a rifle stepped out. He held up one hand and thrust the rifle out with the other.

'You can turn round and go back down — or I can kick your butt hard enough to land you in the next county.'

Drew grabbed the rifle and pulled hard. The man, on the edge of the landing tottered, flailing for balance. By then Drew had a grip on his belt and heaved, quickly stepping to one side as the body blurred past. There was a yell and then a clatter that shook the whole stairway as the guard bounced and rolled and somersaulted to the bottom. He sprawled in the laneway, unmoving.

Drew Hardy quickly stepped through the doorway and a second guard came charging at him, reaching for his Colt. But Drew's Colt came up with a whispering sound, then instantly descended, twice, making muffled thuds as the barrel whipped the man's head. As he sagged, Hardy shoved him out on to the landing, closed the door and slid the inside bolt across.

Denny Clarke, white face drawing twin lines down each side of his mouth in sudden shock, was on his feet behind a desk piled with papers, most tied in bundles with pink ribbon. He was a man in his late fifties, paunchy, skin an unhealthy white. His clothes looked of good quality but he wore them carelessly, and there was cigar ash and spots of what might be wine or food on the front of the silk vest.

Large eyes stared apprehensively at Drew.

'What're you doing here?'

'Came to see you, Denny. Lucky you were doing some overtime. What books're you cooking this time?'

'I resent that!' Clarke snapped, swiftly recovering now as he sat down with a thump in his big leather chair. 'If you're a fugitive, I warn you that I will not hesitate to call the sheriff.'

'Don't make yourself sound more of a fool than you already are, Denny.' Drew dropped into a chair opposite the desk, nursing his Colt casually in his lap. He hooked one boot across his other leg. 'You know exactly when I was released. Guess you were waiting for word from Drago, eh?'

Clarke swallowed but tried to keep his face looking severe. 'I have nothing to do with Drago. In case you've forgotten, he's ramrod of the Lazy H and your brothers — ' He paused. 'Why're you shaking your head?'

'Drago's not ramrod any more — he's nothing. Just fodder for whatever worms that live in the hogbacks.'

The blood drained from Clarke's face again and one hand involuntarily rubbed at his chest. His mouth was open as he gasped for air. 'My God!'

'Hit you where you live, Denny? Well, maybe you better get ready for a few more shocks.'

'What — what're you — ? Look,

Drew, we never hit it off too well, you and me, but I respected Emmett and because of that I'm willing to overlook this — intrusion, and if I can be of assistance in some way — ' He spread soft hands, forced a smile, unsuccessfully. It was more a grimace. 'Just tell me how.'

'Why, thank you, Denny. Right kind of you.'

'Well, as I said — Emmett and me, we did go a long way back.'

'Yeah — you made plenty out of him. Not because you fooled him as often as you figured, but Emmett was a softy underneath that tough shell. He saw you were struggling and he gave you a couple of breaks you obviously weren't aware of — or ignored.'

Clarke flushed, moved restively in his big chair. 'Drew — you have to understand that — well, what information I have concerning Emmett's will and the legal side of the ranch is privileged. In other words — '

'In other words,' Drew cut in bleakly,

'you're all mouth. You don't want to help — only get your butt out of a sling I've put it in. You want me out of here in case I decide to push your face in as well.'

'N-now, hold up!' Denny Clarke rose half out of his chair, one hand pushing air towards Drew.

Hardy suddenly dropped his leg to the floor, the boot slapping hard on the polished tarpaper that showed beneath the edge of the sheepskin rug. He leaned forward so fast that for a moment it seemed as if he would dive across the desk. Clarke practically climbed over the back of the chair.

Drew smiled thinly, leaned both big hands on the desk edge, Colt holstered again now. 'Denny, I want to know about Emmett's will.'

'N-no, no I can't help you there.' The lawyer was shaking his head so fast his jowls quivered. He eased back into the chair, sweat gleaming in the lamp light. 'Except to tell you, you are not a legatee. Even if you were, I still wouldn't,

128

in all conscience, be able to — '

'Denny, there are a lot of things you won't be able to do by the time I'm through here, I give you fair warning. I've had years on that goddamn rockpile and I'm telling you I've got a mighty big pile of my own' — he slapped his head with the heel of his hand — 'in here! Names, deeds, those with me — and those agin me. You savvy what I'm saying?'

Denny nodded very slowly, very positively. 'I — do, Drew, I — do — and I sympathize with you. You got a raw deal and I-I was helpless to do anything for you.'

Drew smiled. 'You mean, you wanted to help me, Denny?'

'Of course I did! I didn't want to see my old friend's youngest son railroaded to Hudspeth — but I had no choice. It was taken out of my hands.'

'Who by, Denny? Who — *by*?'

A dry tongue-tip speared across equally dry lips. 'I — can't tell you that. I'd be violating a trust, not to mention the legal implications — '

Hardy had had enough. He suddenly leapt over the desk, one hand resting on the top, taking his weight while his legs swung up and across. They swept the piles of taped files and papers in a bursting shower and Clarke cowered, arms across his face as he tumbled out of his chair and rolled on the carpet his side of the desk.

Drew bit back the pain in his wound — he had thrust with the left arm instinctively, and he felt wetness under the bandages now. He was reaching down for Denny Clarke's silk vest when a door burst open — in the rear of the room, and the two battered bodyguards limped in, guns in hands.

Damn! He should've figured Clarke would have another entrance — or escape hole!

One of them yelled, the first man he had thrown down the stairs, he thought, all bloody-faced, his clothes in tatters: 'Down, boss!'

He fired his pistol hard on the words

as Clarke rolled beneath his desk, curled up in the knee well. Drew dived for the floor as the second man triggered two fast shots. Glass smashed and a window showered into the room. Drew spun away as the men ran forward. He shot out the lamp and the room was plunged into darkness, except for the burning oil that spilled across the desktop.

Hardy scooped up the sheepskin mat and held it in front of him as he dived out the shattered window. Lead splintered the frame and someone swore bitterly. He felt the glass shards in the frame break loose, but the hide backing of the sheepskin protected him. He kicked as his legs followed his body, hoping he wouldn't drag his flesh across any remaining shards. Luckily he had remembered there was a small balcony running along the front of the building. He almost rolled underneath the rails, kicked back as someone poked his head out, throwing down on Drew with a smoking Colt.

Drew fired his own gun across his body, his lead shattering the already splintered frame above the man. The remains of glass and the collapsing wood fell about the man's shoulders as he backed frantically into the office. Drew ran along the short balcony, climbed on to the landing outside the main door as it burst open and the man he had flung down into the street staggered out, trying to bring up his gun.

'Not your night, *amigo*!' Drew muttered as he hit the man with his shoulder and knocked him once more down the flight of stairs.

This time Drew followed, leaping several steps at a time, hearing Denny Clarke shrieking behind him for someone to help him put out the fire before all his records were lost.

Drew jumped over the battered, groaning guard and ran back through the night to where he had left his horse.

9

Devil's Playground

He made a mistake.

Instead of riding clear of town right away, Drew Hardy went through back lanes he thought he remembered — he got lost twice — and eventually found his way back to Doctor Giles's house.

The medic was surprised, but not too welcoming, as Drew pushed past him, held up his left arm and showed the blood-soaked shirt.

'The devil have you been doing in such a short time? Oh! Of course! We thought we heard shooting. Your doing?'

'Kind of. Doc, I'm heading for the hills and I'm bleeding a bit. Can you fix me up so I won't need to give it any attention for a few days — mebbe a week? I'll — '

Giles held up a hand, led him into

the surgery. 'I don't wish to know what you'll be doing, Drew — I'll patch you up, put a dressing on that you won't need to remove for a few days, even a week. I'll also give you a bottle of antiseptic that you can simply pour over the covering gauze, to keep the infection down, and aid the healing.'

'Obliged, Doc — can you hurry it up?'

Giles shook his head sadly and went about his business. 'You are pushing your luck, young man.'

'Sorry, but that shooting will likely pull the sheriff, whoever he is.'

'Roy Tierney, one of your contemporaries.'

'Hell, how'd *he* get to wear the star! Roy's a fool, always was, even at school. But kind of mean, too.'

When he had finished, Giles had brought him a blue-and-grey checked shirt. 'Left by one of my patients. I think it'll fit.'

Drew was buttoning it up the front when the doctor, cleared his throat. Drew glanced up, paused with a button halfway through the hole when he saw the medic's face.

'Doc — ?'

'Drew — that digitalis. When I noticed its viscosity was thicker than normal, I said to Kerry that there seemed to be a lot less in the bottle than there should've been. He claimed he had knocked it over and spilled some, but that wouldn't account for the remainder being much thicker than the normal tincture.'

'In other words, he lied.'

'I — did notice certain symptoms of overdose in Emmett's hallucinations, disturbed vision, his claims of brightly coloured walls and so on. The actual death was caused by a heart attack which may well have been brought about by an overdose of digitalis. I should've told you before, Drew, but it would be hard to prove — and the implications are very serious.'

'I'm obliged, Doc. I never thought Kerry would go that far . . . '

There was a sudden hammering on

the front door. They exchanged glances.

'Can you delay a minute or two, Doc? My hoss is out the back and — '

'Go, you damn young fool. And good luck.'

He called out irritably that he was coming, got rid of the old bandages and tossed the blood-tinged water down the clay sink. The hammering became more violent.

'Doc! Open up! It's the sheriff — and if you got Drew Hardy in there, you tell him to stay put!'

Giles smiled thinly, shaking his head. *Shouting and giving warning that way was typical of Roy Tierney . . .*

He opened the door, and the sheriff, big and overfed, stood there, wheezing a little, a sullen deputy by his side.

'You surely don't need to make so much blamed noise, Roy — '

The sheriff thrust past the medic and stomped into the infirmary, glanced around, sniffing, waving his six-gun. 'You been treatin' someone! I can smell antiseptic.'

'Yes — Drew Hardy as a matter of fact.'

'What! Where the hell is he? I told you to keep him here and — '

'Long gone, Roy. At least ten minutes before you tried to batter my door down. I was just cleaning up.'

'He hurt bad?'

'Flesh wound — a day or two old.'

Roy's eyes narrowed, almost disappearing as his fat cheeks screwed up. 'Where'd he go?'

'He didn't say: I went to make out his bill and when I returned he was gone — '

'Run out without payin'!' The sheriff nodded in satisfaction as he looked at his silent, stoop-shouldered deputy. 'Somethin' else to nail him with.'

'What's he done?'

'Never you mind, Doc. Enough that you know there's a warrant out for him.' Then he went on, anyway, to tell how Drew had charged into Denny Clarke's, traded lead with the lawyer's bodyguards and set the office ablaze.

'He's just got outta Hudspeth and he'll be back inside two shakes after I catch him! Yeah! An' I ain't forgot the school playground an' how him an' his brothers used to roust me. You sure he never mentioned where he was goin', Doc?'

Giles frowned thoughtfully. 'No-o-o — but he did ask about Rio Concho — general stuff, like, had it changed much in the time he'd been away, were the border patrols still operating . . . '

'Right!' The sheriff rounded fast. He looked smugly satisfied and made for the door, motioning the deputy to follow. 'Headin' for the border, just like I figured. C'mon, Fletch. We'll cut him off at Bowie Pass.'

Doc Giles smiled to himself as he busily tidied up.

Bowie Pass was in the opposite direction to the Sierra Diablos. He hoped that he had assumed correctly that the sierras were where Drew Hardy was making for.

★ ★ ★

That was Drew's planned destination, all right, but his stopping at the infirmary had cost him a deal of time.

He had to move his mount silently and that meant walking it out of town, taking the back alleys again. Once more he became lost, hitting dead ends, or lanes that petered out in weed-grown lots or the bank of the creek that ran across the south end of town. Hangtree had expanded considerably in the years he had been absent, but, finally, he splashed the grey across a narrow section of the creek and mounted on the other side. There was cover here, timber and brush, and a glance at the stars gave him direction.

As he started off, he heard someone shouting — Roy Tierney if he recalled that wheezing, pettish voice correctly.

'C'mon, you men! We'll never make the border by sunup if you don't get a move on! Come *on*, I said!'

Drew smiled thinly, in the deep shadows of the tree. *Good old Roy!* Wearing the sheriff's star sure hadn't given him any more sense. He might as well have stood on top of Mount Livermore, 9,000 feet high, and yelled his intentions . . .

Hardy waited while the small posse Roy had whipped up crossed at the main ford, swung south and cleared town a few minutes later. Then he nudged the grey forward, turned north-east towards the trail to the Diablos.

He hoped he could find Matt Dekker's place again. It was many years since he had seen it — and then only briefly.

★   ★   ★

The delay had been long enough for Denny Clarke to send word to Lazy H that Drew was out of jail and on the prod.

Kerry Hardy, hair standing on end, bleary-eyed from having been rudely awakened by Clarke's messenger, blinked.

'Drew's in town already?' The messenger nodded, started to speak, but stopped as Kerry swore. 'Goddamn! An' he's riled, you say?'

'Well, he busted up Denny's office, set it on fire — but they got it out before too much damage was done. Near killed Buzz Gallen. Threw him down that outside stairway, twice! Shot Bradley. Yeah, I'd say he's some riled.'

Luke had come out on to the porch now, stripped to the waist, wearing a sagging pair of long underpants as sleeping attire. He yawned as he rubbed his eyes.

'He kill Bradley?' The messenger shook his head and Luke grinned. 'That's good — he owes me eleven bucks from last week's poker game.'

'To hell with your damn poker game!' snapped Kerry. 'I wanta know what happened to Drago. Drew mention Drago at all, Mitch?'

'Dunno, Kerry. I was off-duty and Denny drug me outta my bunk an' told me to get out here lickety-split — which I done and, er, I could use a bracer for the ride back . . . '

The Hardys' answer to that hint was to go back into the house — and close the door behind them.

They heard Mitch riding out of the yard as Kerry poured two stiff whiskeys and handed one to Luke.

'He got past Drago, so he must've killed him! *Goddamnit*! Seems Hudspeth's toughened him up.'

'Yeah — an' after all we paid O'Halloran! He din' do the job, bringin' Drew into line with the rest of them convicts, like he said he would: '*I'll break his spirit in a month, boys! Guaranteed*!' Luke spat out the window in disgust. 'Hogwash, the Irish bastard!'

'Not that it matters now, anyway. Drew's a lot tougher than the fools O'Halloran usually has to deal with. Now *we've* gotta deal with the son of a bitch!'

Luke finished his drink and, frowning, refilled his glass. 'He must know somethin', Ker, goin' straight to Denny Clarke that way.'

Kerry nodded grimly. 'That damn

girl! She knew too much: he let her in on too many things just 'cause she could use that typin' machine he bought. Denny should never've fired her the way he did. While she worked there we could more or less control her, at least keep an eye on her — but once Denny kicked her out, she knew he must be suspicious. Now she's gone to ground some place an' we've lost her!'

'We'll lose the ranch if we don't do somethin' about Drew, Ker.'

The older Hardy nodded as he drained his own glass but did not pour another drink. 'Drew might come here!' He smiled slightly as he saw the shock and alarm on his brother's face. 'Well, hell, it was his home — and he knows he's got us to deal with. He'll come and square-up. He was always long on guts.'

'Judas! We better get some of the boys ridin' the fences, watchin' out for him!'

'We'll do better'n that — we'll get 'em watchin' the trail, and put up a big bonus for the one that nails him!' He held out his glass as Luke reached for the bottle again. 'Gimme a refill, we got somethin' to drink to — ' He paused and his grin widened. 'To Brother Drew. May he die with his boots on!'

Luke grinned crookedly, adding, 'An' damn soon!'

★　★　★

The general area was known as the Devil's Playground — a few hundred-or-so desiccated acres of hellfire and thirst, wind-whipped dust to peel a man's skin from his bones, burn his eyes from their sockets. A place of dry, electrical storms as the swirling dust particles collided, giving birth to lightning bolts which struck haphazardly, deadly to animal or human life.

It was a no-go area for any sane person.

Within this main slice of Hell, there was another, smaller area, like an entrée before the main course.

Some folk called it the Devil's

Marbles. By any name, it was a pitiless, parched patch of purgatory, dominated by the twin mounds that gave it its nickname: studded with huge rounded boulders, not an egg-shaped one among the hundreds that clustered in the dry washes and on the flats between the sun-smitten hills. There was not a blade of grass nor any other vegetation; not even a lizard survived here: a barrier to further penetration of the Diablo Sierras. *A warning from the Gods . . . ?*

Drew sat his grey, squinting his eyes against the heat-pulsing glare that made the rocks seem to quiver, despite their size. He could feel the extra heat searing his face, pulled his neckerchief up over his nose and mouth, tugged down his hatbrim to protect his eyes. Each breath burned its way down, scraped his dry throat raw on its journey into his lungs. There was water in his canteen, near-hot water, because of the blistering heat here, but he had to nurture that until he really needed it.

Absently, he moved his shoulder, now

slightly stiff, — wondering if he had been plain loco coming here? But he remembered, long ago, sitting under the shade of the schoolyard's lone oak tree, trading a cold beef sandwich for a home-grown pear with Matt Dekker, wiping juice off his chin as Matt, a tow-haired larrikin with a reckless streak at times, had said, 'Bet I bin a place you never was, Drew.'

Drew had shrugged. 'I ain't been anywhere much — school, ranch, town now and again for supplies, then back to the ranch — and the ranch — and the ranch . . . '

Matt grinned, his small button nose wrinkling. 'Yeah, your old man works your tail off, everyone knows that, but not as hard as he works your brothers. Judas, that Kerry's a mean son of a bitch, Drew! He give you a hard time much?'

'When he figures he can get away with it. Luke'll always back him up an' Emmett gets kinda lost then. Think he knows they're lyin' but don't like to make an issue of it — but he sort of makes things up to me without sayin' that's what he's doin'.' He grinned. 'I don't complain!'

'Yeah, queer feller, your old man.'

'Hey!'

Matt lifted a hand quickly, grinned. 'OK! But this place I been — ' He looked around furtively: none of the other kids was close by, all busy playing lunchtime games. 'Unk came in last week.'

Drew snapped his head up. Unk was Matt's Uncle Wade, a man who rode the edge of the law and had his own small wild bunch out in the Diablo Sierras. He was Matt's hero — in fact, the hero of most boys in Hangtree County.

'Showed up after midnight, bleedin' from a head wound. Ma patched him up an' he told Pa some story about a traitor in his gang, let 'em walk into an ambush by a posse. Pa said he had to get off the spread, pronto, but he's Ma's brother, and she was worried about his

147

wound, said he might fall outta the saddle.'

'Hell!' Drew was wide-eyed, fiercely excited, just being this close to a real outlaw he had only heard about but never seen. 'What happened?'

'Aw, he went all right, but — you know I was off school for a couple days with a bellyache? Well, I wasn't — I never had no bellyache.' He lowered his voice and glanced around furtively once more. 'I rode along with Unk to make sure he got back to his hideout OK!'

'You never!'

'Honest Injun!' Matt held up two fingers close together and touched his right ear.

'Wow! Where is it?'

'Don't think I'd tell, do you! But I'll say this, there's a way through them Devil's Marbles and if you know it, you come out into a little hidden valley, with green grass, a stream, trees an' birds, *everythin'*, slap-bang in the middle of all them sierra badlands!'

Drew had never been sure whether to

believe Matt Dekker or not, but every so often Matt would talk about it, describe a little more. Eventually, when they were nudging their teens and working full time on their parents' ranches, Matt proclaimed, 'I'm gonna find that valley again! Unk's gone now' — Wade was hanged after being caught with someone else's cows — 'an' his gang's scattered. I'm gonna find that valley, Drew!'

'I'll help you look!'

Matt wasn't sure about that, but a few weeks later, with fall starting to bring colder days and nights, he asked Drew to help him get some stores together so they could go on one of their occasional camping trips before the weather turned too cold.

'But we might not hit the usual spots,' Matt said with a wink. 'I think I've remembered the way into Unk's valley . . . '

They had been successful, although it had nearly ended in tragedy with Matt being bitten by a rattler. It was only

Drew's immediate tourniquet and riding him back to Hangtree in a travois Drew made that saved Matt's life. Naturally, the boys had claimed the snake had struck a long way from the Devil's Marbles . . .

Sitting his grey now, Drew wondered if he could remember the way through those boulder fields, across the Devil's Playground.

A lot of years had passed and Matt had eventually followed in the steps of Uncle Wade, unable to resist the temptation to throw a wide loop, or pack in a few kegs of whiskey for the Indians, or even some guns — then hide out in the hidden valley.

Once in a while he would pay some attention to a lonely way station holding a strongbox for the next stage through. Or maybe a stage itself, on one of the lonely desert-skirting trails.

Because there was little or no violence when Matt Dekker pulled-off these crimes, there was a low bounty on his head — $800 was all: he was not held in any great esteem among the law enforcers. Still, he could be a thorn in the side of the stage lines and there was talk of doubling the bounty.

But no one ever found Matt or the few men he led, not only because they retreated to the hidden valley, but they stayed low-key, satisfied with a small income: easy come, easy go . . .

If Lee Dekker had felt she was in any danger, because of what she knew about Emmett Hardy's will, and Denny Clarke's involvement, then hiding out with her brother in that concealed valley would surely be the safest thing for her.

Provided she knew the way.

Drew lifted the reins and touched his heels to the grey's flanks, walking it forward slowly.

After a few yards, he slid Drago's rifle from his saddle scabbard and laid it across his thighs, thumb resting on the hammer spur.

The metal was already hot enough to blister skin.

10

Green Valley

It was sheer bad luck that the Lazy H outrider, young Shelby Goddard, who had plans to become the best broncbuster in Texas, mounted his sorrel on the crest of the small rise at that moment.

He had been checking for tracks of three horses, all mares, that had broken loose from the southern pasture of Lazy H and must've jumped the fence. That told him there was likely some randy wild stallion in the neighbourhood looking for additions to his harem. But the sand was too loose and churned-up without form to give him a good direction. So he mounted and stood in the stirrups, shading his face with his hand, scanning with squinted eyes.

He stiffened as his gaze slid across a

corner of the area known as Devil's Marbles: *dust*, by hell, there was rising *dust*!

Shelby fumbled out the large battered brass field glasses Kerry Hardy had given him to use in his search. Legs quivering as he remained standing in the stirrups, he hurriedly focused, scanned frantically as the field of view was reduced and he briefly lost sight of the dust cloud.

There it was! a slight adjustment to the focus knob and he could see the horse — *and rider!*

Surprise made him drop back into the saddle. He had been prepared to see one of the escaped mares — though he wondered why it would enter such a desolate place — but a rider! 'Hell — alllll-*mighty*!' he breathed in a drawn-out exclamation.

The glasses weren't good enough for him to identify the rider postively, but Shelby, along with every other ranny who worked for Lazy H, had been told to watch out for Drew Hardy — 'wearin' a blue-checked shirt, ridin' a dappled-grey . . . ' Luke Hardy had told them, tight-lipped.

Shelby could make out a blur of blue, and the horse was definitely a grey . . .

The Hardys were offering a hundred bucks and a trip to El Paso for the man who sighted Drew . . .

The money and the prospects of visiting the fleshpots of El Paso were incentive enough for Shelby Goddard to wheel his sorrel and ride hell for leather, back towards Lazy H.

* * *

Blissfully unaware that he had been spotted, Drew rode the reluctant grey in amongst the heat-blasted boulders of the Devil's Marbles.

Landmarks from long ago might have changed but he looked only for the big ones, like the ridge with a broken back almost dead-smack in the middle: a narrow pass.

It was hard on the grey and the horse

whinnied and snorted its protest, made it clear it was obeying only reluctantly, but stepped and staggered on. The cutting narrowed so his knees were almost touching the sides, boots scraping, the horse really nervous and upset now. But it was too narrow to turn so the only way was forward.

Once through, the grey shook its head and mane angrily. But Drew patted its sweating neck, spoke evenly and quietly and it began to calm down . . . in time to face the next section.

This was little better: it passed under a natural arch of rock which was so low he had to dismount and lead the animal through. He smiled grimly to himself as he recalled the devil of a job he had had getting Matt Dekker through here, in the opposite direction on the travois all those years ago . . . It had been touch-and-go that time.

Now, a winding line-thin trail zigzagged down an embankment on to flats that were dappled with clumps of pumice and sharp pieces of basalt. It ended in a hairpin bend that required dismounting again and leading the grey.

It was an ideal spot to place a guard just around the sharp bend, on a natural ledge some ten feet up the side of an otherwise naked, sheer black wall.

Drew froze when he heard a rifle's lever work, even before the rough voice commanded him to 'Stop there!'

Drew looked up, the sun just rimming the high wall, so he couldn't see the man clearly. 'Easy, man! — I'm looking for Matt Dekker.' He sensed he was a half-breed of some kind.

'No heard of him.'

'Then you must be deaf *and* blind, if you live in Hangtree County. There's dodgers on him all over. Actually, it's Matt's sister, Lee, I want to see — I'm Drew Hardy.'

There was silence, then, '*That* name I know. Hang gunrig over saddlehorn — move slow! *No!* Get on other side, away from rifle.'

Drew obeyed, stood back after hanging his bullet belt and holstered

Colt on the saddlehorn, lifted his hands slightly.

'Left arm . . . you hurt?'

'Don't worry — my other one's the gun arm.'

The man laughed briefly. 'Matt say you was a pisser! OK, keep back to me. *Turn around!* That better. Turn head again and I blow it off.'

Drew stood still, felt the man come up close behind him — he had been damn silent climbing down from his ledge! — and then his hat was knocked forward, falling off. He caught it instinctively, hands in front of his chest. And, as he did, a cloth was pulled tight over his eyes and knotted behind his head.

'Now walk — I bring your hoss.'

Drew remembered that the entrance to the valley, under precariously balanced marble boulders, wasn't far from this spot. But he fell maybe ten times going down an incline he didn't remember being so steep. The rifle prodded him to his feet and, holding his hands in front of him, he moved on.

'Stop — right here!'

He obeyed, breathing a little harder than normal, and then the blindfold was yanked off. He blinked, unable to see clearly at first for the cloth had pulled tight across his eyes. Then he saw the valley, aware now he had been hearing birdsong and smelling leaves and wild flowers these past several minutes.

Long and narrow as a knife blade, green as a shamrock, glinting silver marking the creek. It rose steeply on both sides and on the right-hand one, facing east and in a position to catch the first rays of a rising sun, there were two bark-and-log cabins and two crude lean-tos.

Three men stood watching, each holding a rifle. One man moved towards them and by the time he was only a few feet from him, Drew's vision had cleared enough for him to recognize Matt Dekker.

He looked a lot older than Drew

expected, had picked up a bullet scar across his right cheek and the lead had taken a chunk out of his ear on that side. The skin had drawn down permanently, half-hooding his right eye.

'You look a heap better'n I expected,' Matt said, grinning with his stained teeth showing one gap. 'Tougher, meaner, but *fit*.'

'Lots of fresh air and exercise.' Drew grinned and offered his right hand. Matt took it and held firm.

'Damn good to see you again. Was gonna send in one of the boys to bring you if you hadn't found your own way.'

'That damn guard was as good a guide as any.' Drew looked around, but didn't see anyone he thought might be the guard. 'I'm looking for Lee.'

Matt's hooded eye narrowed so that it was almost hidden completely. 'She's here — runnin' scared.'

'That's what I figured when she wasn't around town.'

Matt pointed to one of the tiny cabins up the slope and, as he did, the girl appeared in the doorway, wearing blue shirt and corduroy trousers, a bright scarf around her hair. She recognized Drew and waved.

'I was hoping you'd come,' she said when he walked up and as he drew closer he saw the worry lines on her smooth face.

'Wasn't sure I could find my way in. Never had a chance to thank you properly for getting me to Emmett's funeral. You stuck your neck out there.'

'It just got me mad. I'm kind of impetuous sometimes.'

He grinned. 'You sure are! Tacklin' O'Halloran on his own ground.'

Smiling, she stood aside for him to enter. Inside was essential furnishing, bed, table and chairs, crudely made from tree branches and axe-split logs. Heavy but serviceable — cut-down logs for stools and one attempt at making a chair.

Coffee was brewing at the small fireplace and she poured two cups, brought out some biscuits wrapped in a cloth. 'Left-overs from breakfast. Still quite fresh.'

Drew was hungry and ate three biscuits and drank two cups of coffee. She watched, sipping her own coffee. 'It must feel — good — to be out of that awful place.'

'No complaints. But I stirred up a little trouble with Denny Clarke and his hardcases in town. Roy Tierney's after me.'

Her smiled widened. 'Then you're quite safe.'

Drew grinned. 'Good ol' Roy. All hurry-up and wait.'

'Suits certain people to have him in the sheriff's job *because* he's not too bright.' Beneath the smile and the relaxed manner she tried for, he could detect her tension.

'Why did you start doing things for me? After I went to jail? I mean, we never knew each other that well — usually I only saw you in the schoolyard or sometimes when I came to see Matt.'

Her cheeks coloured. 'Oh, I — well, you were friends with Matt and he didn't make many friends — a shade too tough for most.' She smiled slowly. 'You may recall I used to make you cupcakes, too?'

He nodded, poked his tongue around his mouth. 'Yeah! Still got that tooth I cracked.'

She laughed and he saw the tension drain from her. 'You always — interested me, Drew. Your brothers gave you such a hard time, left you to stand up for yourself, but you always came up smiling. I liked that. And the way you took on all-comers.'

He didn't know what to say: like all schoolboys, he had seen a girl just as someone to poke fun at, even if she was your best friend's sister, and made pretty good cupcakes.

'And then you saved Matt's life and . . . reached hero status as far as I was concerned.' Her cheeks were bright pink now and she busied herself with a blouse button.

Change the subject! he told himself. *Quick!* 'I guess Denny Clarke didn't like you quitting.'

'No — I knew too much about Emmett's wills.' His gaze sharpened. 'The first was quite fair. Emmett divided the ranch between the three of you, but for some reason Kerry and Luke didn't want you to have anything. You being in jail and Emmett with that head injury making him incompetent to attend his own affairs, gave them the opportunity to arrange things to suit themselves.'

'With Clarke's forged power of attorney to help.'

She nodded slowly and he sensed the tension rising in her again. 'You knew about that?'

'Doc Giles mentioned it. Who forged Emmett's hand-writing? Kerry or Luke were never much good with a pen.'

'There was no need. Didn't you notice the typing machine when you were in Denny's office?'

He frowned. 'Saw some kinda black

machine — had a panel with a lot of buttons.'

'It's a typing machine. They've been around for a little while now. Press the right key and it prints that letter on to paper, like a small printing press. I'd learnt how to use one so Denny had me type up the new will he had composed, leaving you nothing, claiming Emmett had said something about you having disgraced the family name, so he was cutting you out of his will entirely. Lazy H went to Kerry and Luke. Denny had no trouble forging your father's signature.'

'You must've known you were in danger after they made you privy to that.'

'I did. I won't bother with details but there were a couple of — incidents — that I felt were designed to scare me, and I *was* scared. I'd known for years how to get to this valley so one night, without so much as a goodbye to anyone, I quit town and made my way here.'

'Good move, Lee. What happened to

the original will? Denny burned it, I suppose.'

'He said he did, but — well, I worked there long enough to know how Denny thinks. I don't believe he would destroy the original. He's more likely to have it hidden somewhere, as his ace in the hole.'

'In case Kerry or Luke decide they can't trust him?'

'I'm sure they don't already, any more than he trusts them. Kerry was in the army with him, so he'll know how risky things are.' She stared into her empty mug. 'I think Denny's holding the original will over their heads. He'll cut himself in for a slice of Lazy H, blackmailing them, threatening to bring out the will unless they give him what he wants . . . '

'Then we gotta get our hands on that original will.'

They turned as Matt came in, holding his rifle.

Drew nodded, but Lee frowned and asked, 'How?'

'You try to figure out where Denny Clarke'd hide it, sis. Then we go in and take it from him.'

'You daren't show your face around Hangtree!' Lee told her brother, aghast at his suggestion.

'Well, with good ol' Roy down on the border lookin' for Drew, I don't see why I can't risk it.'

'It's mighty chancey, Matt,' Drew pointed out.

Matt Dekker shrugged. 'Mebbe, but I never did thank you for savin' my life after that rattler bit me, did I . . . ?'

* * *

Kerry Hardy frowned as he stared at Shelby Goddard, standing before him in the middle of the Lazy H parlour, hat in hand. Before Shelby could say anything, Luke spoke, sprawled in a battered armchair with stuffing showing through several rents in the faded fabric made by his spurs on previous occasions.

'Why the hell would Drew be ridin' into the Devil's Playground? Hell, why would *anyone*? You musta been dreamin', Shell.'

'No, Luke — I seen him through the glasses. Can't swear it was Drew, but whoever he was had on a blue shirt, mebbe with a check, and his hoss was grey.'

Luke grimaced and shook his head. 'Nah — you were mistaken. What you say, Ker?'

'I can't think why Drew would want to ride into that dead ground unless it's to hide out. But he'll want to find out about Emmett's will, so I reckon he's still hangin' around town some place.'

Goddard looked flustered, sure he was right, but afraid to insist to these two hard-eyed ranchers. Instead he took the easy way and backed down. 'I'm sorry, Kerry, Luke. I thought it might've been Drew and you'd want to know.'

'You did right, Shell,' Kerry said. 'Go get yourself a second helping of duff

— tell the cook I said so.'

Goddard grinned and hurried out.

'Kid's eager, ain't he?' Luke opined.

Kerry was still frowning thoughtfully. 'Yeah. But s'pose he was right — and it was Drew?'

'A man'd have to be out of his mind to ride into that hell-place willingly, Ker.'

'Or desperate enough to find somewhere he could hide out and try to figure things. We know Drew's not short on brains, an' he's long on guts. He's got a lot at stake, Luke. He's the kind'll take big risks when he has to, always been that way — part of what the old man admired in him.'

Luke didn't like the way this was going: that Devil's Playground scared the hell out of him, and he felt his belly lurch as Kerry said, flatly, 'We can't risk it! Get your guns — we're gonna have to go in after the son of a bitch!'

11

Night Passage

Drew never thought anyone would try to move across any part of the Devil's Playground at night — let alone *want* to.

'Hell, I only just made it in here — and it was early afternoon when I hit that last trail. Narrow as a pencil stroke,' he told Matt, 'and twisted as an old maid's knitting yarn.'

Matt Dekker grinned. 'You picked the hard way — it's easy enough to defend but we got another exit. Now and again some eager-beaver bounty hunter tries to come into the Marbles your way. No one's made it yet — but you came close.'

'I thought I did make it.'

He looked across at the man who had been on guard when Drew first appeared.

A half-breed Mimbreno Apache, called Tanna. His flat blank expression didn't change but Drew was surprised when one eyelid lowered and rose again.

Drew smiled. 'That's why he blind-folded me.'

'Uh-huh. There's a three-quarter moon tonight, on the wane, but still givin' plenty of light.' Matt heaved to his feet and once again Drew noticed the way he favoured his left side: it had been a tough few years for Matt Dekker and it seemed he hadn't managed to outrun all bullets fired by lawmen or hopeful bounty hunters. 'We'll get movin' — be across the Marbles and down to open country by daylight.'

Lee adjusted the scarf around her hair and tucked her trouser legs into the tops of her high riding boots.

'You're coming?' Drew seemed sur-prised, but it only made sense for her to ride with them — she knew Denny Clarke's office better than anyone, maybe even Denny himself.

'I don't know that I'll be able to find

the will, Drew, but I can think of a few hiding places Denny might use.'

Drew swung his gaze to Matt. 'Who else? Him, I guess' — he gestured to the 'breed — 'and . . . '

'Tanna and Sonny.' Matt nodded towards a grizzled man with grey stubble and a used face with dirt outlining a myriad of wrinkles. He must have been in his fifties, and sure didn't look like anyone Drew would expect to be called Sonny. Matt added, pointing to the other two men squatting outside one of the lean-tos, 'Biggs and Toomey'll stay here. Don't forget to check The Pulpit, boys.'

The smallest man — who happened to be the one named Biggs — lifted a gnarled finger in acknowledgement. Matt smiled as he saw the puzzlement on Drew's face.

'The Pulpit's a needle rock halfway up the slope of what we call the Gateway — got a good sized chunk of a saloon mirror planted up there — an' don't ask which saloon or how we come by it. Man with another mirror knows just where it is and can hit it with a beam of sunlight to give a pre-arranged signal.'

'No wonder no one ever found you.'

'Was one of Unk Wade's better notions. Now let's saddle up and ride.'

★ ★ ★

Neither Kerry nor Luke liked the idea of entering the Devil's Playground at night.

They had brought Shelby Goddard along together with two hardcases who had done jobs for the Hardys over the years and had been well-paid to keep their mouths shut: Lonnie Carl and Whitey Norris.

Shelby wasn't keen on going into that country at night but he led the way to where he had seen the horseman he thought could've been Drew Hardy riding into the area of Devil's Marbles.

Silver light lay across the land like a woman's wispy shawl but strong enough to throw distinct shadows. Goddard stopped on the ledge and pointed.

'I was here, boss, an' the rider was movin' past the last of them needle rocks before the Marbles begin.'

'How the hell could you see him?' Luke demanded, suspiciously. 'There's a solid line of rocks an' Drew's no dummy. He'd've rode on the far side, used 'em as a screen.'

'Well, Luke, that ain't a line of rocks you're seein',' Goddard said, his voice nervous as always when he had to contradict one of the Hardys. 'That's solid shadow right now, several shadows in one block. See the angle of the moon? You can make out the needles agin the stars . . . '

'All right, all right!' growled Luke, annoyed he had made such an elementary mistake. 'So you seen him — ridin' which way?'

Goddard pointed, his hand trembling slightly, and drew an imaginary line. 'That direction — I lost him when he angled far enough round to be screened by the rocks.'

'An' never thought to follow him!' Luke growled again, glad to have some reason to pick on the hopeful young wrangler. 'With rocks like that for cover, you could've picked him off an' — '

'I ain't no bushwhacker!' broke in an outraged Goddard, surprising himself at his tone of denial. ''Sides, Kerry said the bounty'd be paid for *sightin'* Drew. No one said nothin' about tryin' to trade lead with him.'

'You be lucky to have a job by the time this is over, you sassy sonofa!'

'Forget it!' snapped Kerry. 'Quit the goddamn raggin', Luke. Shell's here just to show us where he last saw Drew. What he might've done, don't count.'

Luke snorted, 'Well, I ain't goin' in there in this light. You wanna, go ahead. I'll camp out here till you come back. *If* you do!'

Kerry threw him a cold look. 'We *all* camp here. No sense in tryin' to find a way in there now. But we'll have an early start come morning.'

'Fine with me.' Luke yawned. 'Ain't used

to bein' up this late, 'less I got someone like Ginger La Salle to keep me company.'

Shelby Goddard's eyes flew open at mention of the most expensive whore in Hangtree County. 'You been with — *her*? Honest Injun . . . ?'

'Hell, lotsa times,' bragged Luke, glad of the small audience as Lonnie Carl and Whitey Norris edged closer. 'What makes her so expensive is she's got this trick she does with her — '

'For Chris'sakes! Will you two shut *up*!' snapped Kerry. 'Save your dirty talk for the bunkhouse and get our bedrolls set up amongst these rocks. Luke, you seem set to do some dreamin' so you got first watch.'

'The hell I have. Give it to Shelby.' He laughed briefly. 'I'll tell him just enough about Ginger to keep him awake all night thinkin' of it . . . '

'Just — get — it — done!'

Kerry wanted to yell, all on edge, not in the least looking forward to venturing into the Devil's Playground come daylight.

But it was a chance, maybe the only chance, of getting Drew and putting him out of the Lazy H picture — permanently.

★   ★   ★

Drew was mighty glad to have guides through this terrible land.

Matt and his men knew it well, thanks to Unk Wade and Tanna's knowledge from when he was with his long-vanished tribe. Drew instinctively tightened his grip on the grey's reins when he saw some of the rugged country looming ahead.

But Tanna, without hesitating, led the way through some convenient path between jutting rocks or found a natural bridge over a deep narrow canyon that fell away abruptly. It necessitated careful riding and, to make it safer, Matt ran a line from the lead rider, Tanna, back to each of the others following. They just had to keep a light touch on the grass rope and follow the tugs or twists or sometimes slackness.

It was a new experience for Drew, negotiating trails as dangerous as these at night: without the aid of the moon he doubted he would have tried it. No, without Tanna none of them would have tried it.

He was surprised when they came to a flat ledge wide enough for them all to assemble while still mounted. The horses were sweating and blowing, none of them entirely at ease, though he figured his grey and Lee's sorrel were the two most anxious.

Matt Dekker gazed at the moon, tipped over and riding a downward curve towards the ragged outlne of the mountain chain, and announced, 'We rest here for an hour — that way it'll be just before daylight when we get through the Marbles.'

He saw Drew's frown and smiled crookedly. 'Reckon it'd be better to arrive in full dark?'

'Was thinking that Roy's posse's s'posed to be down on the border at

Rio Conchos, but there's no guarantees. He's dumb, but he'd likely figure I might try to hide out in here if he was convinced I'm not in that border country.'

'Roy's dumb but he has flashes of smart. No, not worried about him. Worried about us. The way we have to leave this neck of the woods is by a mighty narrow trail clingin' to the outside of that run of needle rocks, on the side away from the approaches that'll give us cover. We need just enough light to see.'

Drew shrugged. 'Your bailiwick — but seems a lot harder than that trail I took in.'

'Not really, cos it gives you that cover I spoke of. Reverse the way you rode in and suddenly you clear the Marbles and there you are — a fine target outlined agin all that sandstone, and your hoss'd have to pick its way down in a slow zigzag. Unk Wade drilled it into me. It's why he managed to hang out in there for so long.'

'Mighty careful — and you have to admire him, hiding out in here all those years. You aiming to break his record?'

Matt chuckled. 'Got so many aches and pains from old wounds and it feels like rheumatics are already catchin' up with me, sleepin' out for so long. No, not tryin' for a record. We're workin' on one final big job and then we'll scatter.'

Drew frowned. 'Watch out for that last big chore, Matt. Half the population of Hudspeth are fellers who figured one final job'd set 'em up for life. They got 'life' all right, but not the kind they wanted.'

'Hey! You tryin' to worry me? Thought you had more faith in me than that.'

'Was inside too long, I guess.'

'If you can't find that will, and Kerry and Luke won't give you your rightful share of Lazy H, look me up — I'll gladly cut you in on a few jobs — get some practice before we run the big one. We'll retire together. There's this widder I know, runs a big *rancho* down

179

in Sonora, got four young daughters . . . '

'Let's see how we make out here.'

'Sure.' Matt Dekker nodded, but frowned a little: he should've known better. Nothing would keep Drew from getting back what was rightfully his.

* * *

'No fires!' Kerry snapped angrily, kicking the kindling the squatting Luke was about to light. It scattered and Luke sat down with a hard thud, spilling his matches. He glared up at his brother as he climbed to his feet, dusting-off.

'Goddamnit, Ker! What the hell?'

Kerry leaned forward slightly from the hips. 'No — damn — fires, you blamed idiot!'

Luke knew it had been stupid, but he was only half awake, had put himself to sleep sipping a bottle of Wild Turkey bourbon. But he resented being treated like some dumb cowhand. 'I need coffee!'

'Chew a handful of beans then, you need a lift bad enough — but there'll be no fires. We're not on a goddamn picnic.'

'Kerry!'

The rancher stopped speaking and rounded swiftly on Lonnie Carl, but the angry words died unspoken as his gaze automatically followed Lonnie's pointing arm.

Kerry Hardy froze, and Luke, standing up now, stiffened as he, too, saw what Lonnie was pointing at.

A smudge of dust, highlighted amongst the Devil's Marbles, *behind* the visible boulders.

'There ain't no trail in there!' Luke allowed.

Kerry frowned, studying the rising dust cloud. 'No animal life in there, either, that'd raise dust like that. Gotta be riders!'

'I don't see how — ' Luke let his words break off as Whitey Norris, who had climbed up on to a narrow ledge, hanging virtually by his fingertips, called down in his womanish voice.

'By God! It's riders, all right! Looks

like — four — no *five*! An' one of 'em's a woman!'

'Lee Dekker!' breathed Kerry and it was more a prayer than a mere announcement. 'Hell, if that's Matt — and Drew, if he's found his way to them — boys, hunt some cover! They'll have to come past this way an' we got the best position we coulda wanted!'

He couldn't resist crowing just a little as he looked into Luke's incredulous face.

'Now, ain't you glad I kicked them matches outta your hand?'

'Ask me after I get Drew in my sights!'

★   ★   ★

Tanna stayed in the lead, riding now with his rifle butt on his thigh, right hand gripping the throat of the stock, a finger lightly on the trigger. The hammer was cocked and the dark eyes restlessly roved over the surrounding landscape.

Drew and Matt followed, with Lee

riding beside her brother, looking tired and a little nervous. Sonny brought up the rear, a shotgun across his thighs.

The light was increasing swiftly as the horizon brightened, the sun straining to climb above the mountains. Shadows moved as the light washed in waves through the broken land, but these were low down, at ground level.

Drew saw something move higher up one wall, hipped quickly and next instant his Colt was roaring in his hand, making the horses leap and snort with its suddenness. Lee stifled a startled cry as the two shots blended into one slapping echo. She saw a man's body fall from a narrow ledge, bounce off a jutting rock and then sprawl unmoving on his back. A rifle clattered down after him and before it came to rest, leaving a small dust trail, Drew's gun thundered again and he whirled the grey in front of Lee's sorrel, yelling, 'Hunt cover!'

Even Tanna hadn't seen the shadow that gave Drew Hardy warning and he whirled now, bringing his rifle across as

Sonny's shotgun thundered through the morning. The buckshot ricocheted like whistling birds, scarring a boulder with silver. A man swore, but it was more of a grunt than a cry of pain. Drew figured one of the buckshot balls had creased him, whoever he was.

Other guns opened up from behind other rocks, and one on the ledge, this one firing desultorily. Shelby Goddard was prepared to join in the shooting now it had started, but he had made damn sure he wasn't the one to fire the first shot. He was still green and young enough to have strange notions about giving a man a chance before busting a cap on him.

Kerry and Luke and the surviving hardcase, Norris, were raking the group below, although Matt's band had scattered, hunting cover. Sonny never made it: he whipped around in the saddle, shotgun reloaded, and held it in both hands as he raised it towards the ledge.

Luke Hardy half rose from where he

was crouching, sighted quickly and slammed a bullet into Sonny's narrow chest. Sonny convulsed as he triggered, the shotgun leaping from his grip as it discharged. The recoil spun the weapon and it slapped Lee's snorting, frightened sorrel across the head. The horse staggered, whickering shrilly, reared, and Lee lost her grip, tumbling from the saddle.

Matt called her name and wrenched his own mount's head around to lunge back towards her. Drew fired and saw Luke stumble back and drop out of sight, clawing at his face.

Lying low over the stretched-out grey, Drew levered a shell into his rifle's breech, leaned lower and fired one-handed under the horse's arching neck. Whitey Norris staggered even as he fired and, as he fought for balance, Tanna shot him through the head, his hat flying off, white hair suddenly splashed with crimson as he was hurled from the rocks.

Drew pulled himself back into the

grey's saddle, looking around for Kerry: he couldn't see his brother anywhere and this worried him. This ambush had all of Kerry's touch and he knew the man would be somewhere he could get in the best shot — and at the same time command the best protective cover.

But there was no sign of him.

Tanna's old rifle jammed, a shell trapped in the worn ejector. He was fighting it, holding on with his knees, when a bullet punched him sideways and backward. He bounced off his mount's rump and hit the ground rolling and tumbling.

Drew twisted violently, spotted Luke, his face bleeding in a dozen places from rock chips, levered and fired, but missed. Levering again, he glanced around for Matt Dekker — and saw the man's horse had stopped running, stood panting beside a large boulder, with Matt leaning one shoulder against the rock, arm hanging loosely, his gun slipping from weakened fingers, mouth hanging slackly.

Raging, Drew spun back towards the bushwhackers' ledge but froze as Kerry's voice yelled through the swirling clouds of gunsmoke:

'Just drop the rifle, Drew! You can see where mine's pointing!'

Drew hipped round more, froze.

Kerry was standing over a dazed and dusty Lee Dekker, his cocked rifle pressed against the back of her head.

Drew's Winchester thudded to the dust as he raised his hands slowly to shoulder level.

Full daylight blazed across the Devil's Plaground as the heavy pall of gunsmoke shredded in the barely eddying breeze, already stifling.

12

Family Ties

Lee was coming out of her daze, but froze when she tried to move her head and felt Kerry's rifle muzzle pressing into her neck. She heard him chuckle and then a hand grabbed her shoulder and squeezed hard enough to make her gasp.

'Stand up!' He jerked at the same time and she had no choice but to get her shaky legs under her and stagger to her feet. He shoved her roughly towards a boulder and told her to sit down — on her hands.

Lee complied, tight-lipped, looking past him to where Drew sat his saddle, still with hands raised, face set in hard lines, narrowed eyes watching Kerry closely. The oldest Hardy brother came towards him slowly.

'Luke!' Kerry called as he approached, not taking his gaze off Drew. 'Luke! You make it?'

A few stones clattered and then Luke stumbled out of the rocks, face streaked with blood and matted dust. Shelby Goddard, white-faced, steadied him and helped him down. Angrily Luke shook free and spat, brought up his rifle swiftly as if he would shoot Drew.

'No!' snapped Kerry. 'Watch the girl: you, too, Shell.' Luke swore softly but edged over towards the girl, limping a little. Drew saw a small patch of blood on his trousers and guessed he had been clipped by a bullet or had hurt himself when he fell amongst the rocks.

Shelby Goddard looked mighty uncomfortable as he leaned down and asked Lee if she would like a hand up. She smiled, but Luke pressed her down with his rifle barrel.

'Stay put. You go find the horses, kid.'

Goddard looked glad of the chance to get away from this unfolding drama. Kerry looked up at Drew and smiled thinly, rifle covering him. 'Come on down, little brother — I got a chore for you.'

'I've got something else for you,' Drew said, hardly moving his lips but Kerry only grinned wider, shaking his head, supremely confident he was in charge.

'Get down! And keep your hands raised all the time.'

It made it awkward for Drew to dismount that way, and he swung his left leg a couple of times before he managed to hook it around the saddle horn, shifted weight on his buttock, upper body swaying.

Luke guffawed. 'Like old Moonshine Monaghan on a bender, ain't he?'

Kerry laughed, nodding.

Then suddenly he had his arms full of Drew Hardy.

Drew used the saddle horn as a lever for his body, kicked his right boot free of the stirrup and launched himself at the startled Kerry. His weight carried them both to the ground and Kerry lost the rifle. Then Drew's knee caught him alongside the jaw and a fist hammered the side of his head.

Kerry yelled and bucked and twisted and rolled, not still for a second, knowing the moment he froze Drew would have the upper hand completely. All Kerry's writhing unsteadied Drew and he put down one hand to keep from sprawling. Kerry, snake-quick, knocked it from under him and as Drew fell he slid out, rolled away, bouncing quickly to his feet. He saw Luke crouching, rifle ready in both hands, looking for an opening to shoot at Drew.

'Just watch the girl!' Kerry snapped and literally jumped in as Drew started to straighten. His boot caught Drew on the shoulder although it had been meant for his jaw. It spun him and he hit the dust again.

Drew skidded and rolled and kept rolling twice more before bouncing up to meet Kerry's charge. Kerry wasn't expecting that and tried to stop and then swing to one side. He lost control of his balance, swayed and threw his arms wide to compensate.

That left him wide open and Lee, crouched against the boulder with Luke once again standing almost on top of her, heard Drew's fist thud into Kerry's neck, and then an upper cut that clacked his teeth together. Kerry's arms flung wide again, but not under his control this time: it was his body's instinctive motion, an attempt to keep him upright. But Drew's punches had been powerful and he only stumbled, went down to one knee.

Drew stepped in, lifted a knee into Kerry's face. The man crashed backwards and did a half somersault before toppling to one side. His hand closed over gravel and he came up fast, hurling it into Drew's face as he advanced.

Drew jerked his head aside but felt the sting of small, sharp-edged stones down one side of his face. Then, before his vision was entirely clear, two pile-driving blows shook him, making his ribs creak. He felt his wound tear open a little and the sharp, dagger-like pain set his juices roaring through him.

Kerry closed. Drew stepped to meet him. Both men's bodies jarred and shuddered under a flurry of blurred, grunting hammer-blows. Kerry bared his teeth with effort or hate — or both — turned a shoulder into Drew and swung a roundhouse right that fairly whistled. If it had landed it would have taken Drew's head off.

But it didn't land. Drew dropped to one knee and, as Kerry stumbled to retain his balance, sank a fist almost to the wrist in his brother's mid-section. Kerry gagged and stopped, for a moment, hanging, doubled-over, on the end of Drew's fist.

Then his youngest brother stepped back, his other fist coming in and hooking Kerry on the jaw. The man's feet left the ground and he crashed on to his side in the dust, spitting blood, eyes rolling up in their sockets.

Drew was gasping for breath, spread

his legs to steady himself, then moved in to finish Kerry.

'*Drew!*'

He vaguely heard Lee's warning, started to turn. All he saw — or glimpsed — was the butt end of Luke's rifle coming towards him. It thudded between his eyes and everything went black.

So quickly, he didn't even remember falling.

$$\star \quad \star \quad \star$$

His hands were bound behind him when he came to — slowly, painfully, head feeling as if it had been split like a roofing shingle, pulse-pounding behind his eyes, disturbing his vision.

He was still at the edge of the Devil's Marbles.

It came into focus slowly. His mouth was dry, throat aching for cool water, jaw stiff. Even his teeth were acting up, feeling as if they had all been pulled.

'Here.'

Drew started as the warm metal neck of a water-bottle was pressed to his swollen lips. He gulped, feeling some spill over his chin, run down his neck. Then it was withdrawn and he saw it was Kerry, kneeling beside him, now capping the canteen.

'That's the last bit of comfort you can expect from me, Drew.'

'Glad of it, anyway,' he managed to rasp as he glanced around. 'Where is she?'

'With Luke and the kid — they took her — somewhere.'

That was the kind of thought Drew needed to jar him back to full reality. He tried to stretch his wrists against his bonds, uselessly, but having to try anyway.

'What're you going to do with her? She's not in this. Matt just brought her along. Where is he, anyway?'

'Matt?' Kerry gestured casually over his shoulder without looking around. 'Tumbled off his horse in those boulders. Don't worry about him

195

— he's dead — might even put in a claim on the reward for him, miserable as it is.'

Drew's battered face hardened and he saw Kerry involuntarily rear back an inch or two when he saw Drew's eyes.

'Don't get any ideas, little brother — I control you now.'

'News to me.'

Kerry laughed, then grimaced, grabbing his throbbing swollen jaw, a little blood oozing from a cut on his upper lip. Then his hand lashed out as he backhanded Drew, turning his brother's head violently to one side.

'You son of a bitch! I could always whip you!'

Drew smiled, even as blood oozed from a corner of his mouth. 'Not this time — Luke saved your neck.'

Kerry hit him again, standing now, nostrils flaring as he glared down. He kicked Drew in the side. 'I've had a bellyful of you! All them years, Emmett favouring you over me and Luke! Hell, we built Lazy H! The old man drove us like a couple swamp-runnin' slaves! We thought he was hard, but after you come along — ' He paused, breath hissing through his partly open mouth, as he leaned down. 'You shouldn't even be here! You was an accident! Hell, I'm ten years older'n you! Luke's got eight or nine on you! That damn Evie, as Pa used to call her, was forty-somethin' when you come along. That's how come you killed her: it was too late for her to be whelpin'! Blame the wild old man, I guess: it sure changed him.' He snorted. 'If we thought he was hard before you was born . . . Hell, that was a picnic! Once he seen how much you resembled Evie, and his conscience troublin' him over her dyin' giving birth to you — man! We had years of whippin's 'n the back of his hand long before you was old enough to wipe your own nose! Then we had all that time watchin' him favour you with schoolin', and takin' you everywhere with him while we busted our asses on Lazy H.' Worked-up, he slapped Drew back and forth, back and forth, with his hand. Drew's cheeks turned scarlet, white lines marking the passage of Kerry's fingers and knuckles. 'You din' earn no share of Lazy H, you spoilt bastard! An' Luke and me are gonna make sure you never do get a share.'

'Thought you already had — by having Denny Clarke fake the will so only you and Luke get the spread.'

Kerry smiled bleakly. 'Uh-huh. Yeah, figured that gal'd tell you. Well, that's as maybe. *I'll* tell *you* somethin' now: Denny Clarke wants a share of Lazy H, a big share — to sell off to a railroad that's gonna link El Paso, Sierra Blanca and Van Horn! You b'lieve it? That sneaky, son of a bitch has got the inside runnin' to somethin' like that, part of *our* legacy! And he's holdin' the original will over us. Do what he says, or when he's ready, he'll tie everything up by producin' the other will, the one Emmett made before he had that fall — and leavin' half the spread to you.'

Drew stiffened. 'I thought it was

equal shares, you, Luke and me?'

Kerry shook his head. 'No — *half* goes to you; Luke and me divide what's left between us. Just one lousy *quarter* each! Judas! That old man really stuck it to us!'

'Lee said it was a third each.'

'Then Lee was wrong.' He paused, frowned. 'Or was she? Denny never let us see the damn will — wonder if he just told us you got the lion's share so we'd agree to him forgin' a new one? He's kept the old one as a hold over us.'

'What's it matter? You and Luke are running things the way you want.'

'But Denny still has the original!' Kerry was frowning deeply now. 'We gotta get a look at it, more'n ever now.' He dropped his gaze to Drew. 'And you're gonna get it for us, Drew — I mean you *better* get it.'

'I want to see it just as bad as you, Kerry.'

'Mebbe. But it won't do you no good, tell you that now. What you smilin' about? Think you'll just refuse to go get it? Or turn it over to some smart-ass lawyer, mebbe, in El Paso?'

'Told you I want to see it. But if I get it, I don't necessarily have to show it to you.'

'Wrong, little brother.'

Kerry dropped to one knee again so he looked more or less levelly into Drew's battered face.

'You're gonna get that will, and kill Denny Clarke while you're doin' it, then bring it straight back to Luke and me.'

Drew stared, gaze steady, trying to figure why Kerry sounded so confident he would do what he wanted.

Then he stiffened, drew in a sharp breath and Kerry laughed.

'Figured it out, huh? Yeah — you bring me that will or Lee Dekker gets chopped up a little at a time till you do.' He stood up, still grinning. 'When I was a medic in the War, they taught us how important the old thumb is to us humans — more so than fingers. Lose a finger, you can still do most things.

200

Lose a thumb — well, you try loading a rifle or openin' a door with just four fingers — ain't easy, and there's a hundred jobs you'll never be able to do again without a thumb to help give you a proper grip. Then, you start losin' fingers as well, you're in real trouble.'

He shrugged, smile widening as he saw the savage anger building behind Drew's eyes. 'That's it, Drew. You bring the will to me soon's you get it, *after* you kill Denny, of course — or Lee Dekker loses a thumb. She's got two thumbs, not to mention eight fingers. Hell! Almost forgot — *ten toes*! Two ears, enough hair to stuff a pillow — she sure could be one helluva mess if you decided to hold on to the will.'

Drew looked and felt murderous, writhed and tugged futilely at his bonds. If he could get free, he knew he would kill Kerry, brother or not, right now . . .

And Kerry was amused, almost jovial.

'Just in case you got some notion of

201

jumping me when I turn you loose so you can head for town — Luke knows if I don't show by a certain time, then I likely ain't gonna show at all an' he knows just what to do. He's impatient, Luke is, as you likely know. Recollect how he was always first to the candy counter, kickin' and bitin' his way past everyone? Sure you do. And you know how mean he can be.' Kerry laughed suddenly. 'You ought to see your face!'

'I'd rather see yours — over my rifle sight.'

Kerry, grinning, just shook his head. 'Never happen, Drew.'

'What happens after I bring you the will?'

Kerry shrugged. 'Go wherever you like — there'll never be anythin' here for you. See? I've really got you whipped this time, little brother!'

* * *

Shelby Goddard watched as the three ranch hands swinging the new barn

202

door stopped work to stare at the trio riding into the Lazy H yard.

Frowning, licking his lips, he turned to look past the dishevelled girl on her sorrel to Luke bringing up the rear, his rifle across his thighs. The kid rode back alongside Hardy.

'What we gonna do with Miss Dekker, Luke?'

Luke turned his mean eyes to the young rider's concerned face. 'Keep her here till Drew gets back from Hangtree with Emmett's will.'

The girl was watching them closely now, face smeared with dirt, hair awry where it showed beneath her hat. Her shirt was torn on one shoulder and a riding boot was badly scuffed, one knee of her corduroy trousers ripped. She should have looked hangdog and pathetic, but there was a defiant tilt to her head and the small jaw, though bruised, looked formidable to Shelby.

'But *where* we gonna keep her, Luke?'

'Tack room, mebbe, or the old root

cellar. Have to fix the door first, but — '

'Judas, there's rats in there! Might be snakes gone in after 'em.'

He saw the uncertainty in Lee's eyes at his words and could have bitten his tongue. Luke grinned, watching Lee.

'Thanks, Shell — nice timin', huh, Lee?'

She said nothing but Shelby Goddard was glad he wasn't on the receiving end of the kind of look she threw at Luke Hardy.

'There's that spare room off the kitchen, Luke,' the young cowboy said quickly. 'The one I stayed in till there was a bunk for me in the main bunkhouse.' He turned to Lee. 'It's kinda cramped, and only has a stretcher-bunk but — '

'Shut up, kid. And go tell them gawkin' idiots to get on with swinging that barn door. I'll take care of Miss Uppitty here. It ain't your worry.'

Goddard still hesitated, teeth tugging at his lower lip. He glanced at Luke's hard face, then lowered his gaze, muttering, 'I'm sorry, ma'am.'

'So am I, Shelby — but thank you.' Lee looked at Luke. 'Put me where you like. Drew'll find me when he's ready.'

Luke's mouth twisted as he scoffed. 'You think he's comin' for you? Judas, the moment he hands over that will to Kerry, he's a dead man.'

Lee was shocked. 'For Heaven's sake! He's your *brother*!'

She was sick to her stomach and felt all the hope she had been holding drain away as if someone had pulled a plug.

'So what?' Luke said carelessly.

13

Legacy

Still with his wrists bound, Drew Hardy watched impassively as Kerry worked on his rifle and Colt before letting him have them for the ride into Hangtree and the recovery of the will.

Kerry was taking no chances.

He disassembled the Colt, removing the cylinder and stowing it in the bottom of Drew's left-hand saddle-bag. The frame of the six-gun he buried deep in Drew's right-hand saddle-bag, ripping open a bag of coffee grounds so they spilled into the works. The ammunition, including the shells shucked from the belt loops, he scattered amongst spare clothing in Drew's bedroll, then strapped it back behind the saddle.

He ejected all the shells from the rifle, pushed one shell halfway into the breech, then deliberately worked the lever, jamming the shell in the ejection port.

'Take you some time to set yourself up again with your guns,' Kerry told him, pointing out the obvious. He grinned tightly. 'By that time, I'll be long gone — but I'll be watching my back trail, in case you got any loco notions of coming after me instead of Denny Clarke.'

'I think you're scared of me, Kerry.'

The oldest Hardy brother froze as he picked up the rifle cartridges, rounded fast. 'Scared of you? Hell, look at you — trussed like a hog for the cookin'. *I'm* the one walkin' free.' He tossed the handful of shells into the bushes, scattering them. 'I'm just being smarter than you, Drew boy, and if you're smart, you won't waste no time in getting along the trail to town.'

He went to his horse and mounted. 'You'll be able to work free from them ropes in time. See you at the ranch, sometime tonight — OK?'

'No.' Drew's abrupt objection brought

Kerry upright in the stirrups, eyes narrowing as he dropped a hand to his gun butt. 'You bring Lee here — I'll be waiting with the will. *Shut up*, Kerry! Do it that way or put a bullet in me now.'

Kerry's face was like stone in the shadow of a thunderhead as he drew and cocked his Colt, aiming it at his brother. He lowered the hammer slowly, 'Wouldn't do Lee any good, not one bit. So, you come — '

'Here!' cut in Drew, heart hammering, knowing full well the chance he was taking. 'I'll bring the will *here*. If you're not waiting, then you better post plenty of guards, because I'll be coming after you.'

Kerry remained rock-sober a moment longer, then holstered his gun. He laughed, shaking his head. 'You mule-headed son of a bitch! You might look a lot like your ma, but by hell, you're as obstinate or worse than old Emmett!'

Drew waited, expressionlessly.

Kerry snorted suddenly and walked

his horse over Drew, forcing his younger brother to writhe and twist so as to dodge the hoofs. 'Just get that will!'

Kerry was still chuckling when he disappeared from sight.

Drew swore softly, looked around, rolled and pulled himself along using his heels to get his body in close to some rocks he had noted earlier. They had obviously rolled down from above, undermined by the winds probably, and two had shattered when they came to rest. He grunted and heaved around until his bound wrists were against one of the ragged edges of a split. But the rock was too unsteady, moved and shifted when he put pressure on and tried to rub the ropes up and down along the sharp edge.

The next one he tried was better, wedged tightly on its side. It meant he had to lie supine, so as to get the ropes between his wrists to move back and forth along the horizontal sawtoothed stone. Some fragile points broke off.

Others, ragged and tough, tore at his skin and blood flowed.

He was leery of cutting the arteries in his wrists but he forced his hands apart, stretching the fibres, until, strained to the limit, they snapped one by one. At last his hands were free, but they were so numbed he didn't realize it at first. His upper arms and shoulders ached intolerably, specially the wounded one.

He lay there, gasping from his efforts — must have taken an hour's work, he figured, glancing at the position of the sun. He used his now tingling hands to rub circulation into his forearms. His grey was ground-hitched nearby and he crawled across, pulled himself upright by the docile animal's left foreleg and fumbled for the saddle canteen. The water was tepid but slaked his huge thirst. He hesitated, then poured some over his matted hair and rubbed it across his face, getting rid of some of the grit and grime.

He felt ready to tackle his warbag and saddle-bags and get his weapons in firing condition. Even after all that time in Hudspeth, where there were, of course, no guns to handle, he did the job in record time, his hands seeming to move of their own accord in the correct sequence so that there was little fumbling, only rapid, near-expert assembly. He had to use some more precious water to clear the coffee grounds from the six-gun but that was the only real problem. He found enough cartridges in the brush to load up the rifle.

Tearing a corner off his shirt-tail, he moistened it and wrapped it around his left wrist where it had been cut fairly deeply by the sandstone. Then he mounted and was ready to hit the trail to Hangtree when he remembered Matt Dekker.

Kerry had casually indicated some rocks where he had said Matt had crawled to die. Drew rode the grey across, dismounted and searched for his old friend.

He found him, slumped against a rock, head hanging at an awkward angle, eyes half open. But he was dead — and not from the wounds he had taken during the ambush. They were serious and had bled a good deal, but Drew figured Matt would have been tough enough to survive them.

But not the fresh bullet hole in his right temple, the skin and short hair all singed and blackened by the powder flash as the gun muzzle was pressed in hard.

A deliberate, cold-blooded killing shot.

Drew straightened, his jaws aching, he clenched his teeth so hard.

It scared him a little to realize how eager — and willing — he was at this moment to kill his own brothers. It didn't matter which one had done it; both had had the chance to do it it and, worse, he realized suddenly, either was capable of such a cold-blooded murder of a helpless man.

★　★　★

He wasn't sure if Roy Tierney and his posse had returned to Hangtree so he entered by a roundabout route, leaving his mount in a weed-grown lot behind the main drag. On foot, he made his way towards the law office: no horses in the stables — a good sign. Hand on the six-gun butt he hunched down along the side of the building. He took off his hat and, rubbing a little dust from window glass just above the bottom of the frame, looked inside.

There was a man in there, but a second look showed him the man had his feet up on the desk and was asleep in the big chair, gnarled hands folded across his skinny midriff.

'Pop' Candsale had been old even when Drew was a boy — or it had seemed that way. Pop was a jack-of-all-trades, collected some kind of pension from one of the stage lines after having been wounded while successfully defending the strongbox. He earned a little extra by swamping the saloons, helping in the general store and freight shed and caretaking the law office when the sheriff was out of town.

Staying hunched over, Drew made his way to Main, turning away from the law office and going down to the lane where Denny Clarke had his offices.

Drew had succesfully unjammed his rifle but hadn't brought the weapon with him, knowing there was the steep, narrow stairway to negotiate before he could enter the small office area: a rifle would only cramp his style once in that small space.

Drew figured Denny Clarke would have replaced the two bodyguards he had met earlier: Buzz and Bradley. He worked his right hand, massaging it, as it still felt a little numb and ached from the long time his wrists had been bound.

No use putting it off, so he started up the stairs as quietly as he could but figured someone up there would know he was coming. Four steps from the top, he suddenly lunged, using his left hand on the rail to give him more impetus. He turned his right shoulder as he hit the door.

It jarred in the frame but didn't open. Drew lifted his right leg and kicked at the lock, full weight behind it. Wood splintered and he used his shoulder again on the upper panel. The door slammed inwards — but there was no crashing clatter as it struck the wall. Instead, a man groaned sickly and staggered out from behind it, where he had been flattened against the wall, aiming to jump Drew as he entered.

Hardy went in, shoulder-rolling across the floor and a gun banged. He saw the flash from the shadows, glimpsed a man lifting his smoking pistol again. Drew, on his back, triggered, and the man slammed back, struck a desk and rolled off. By then Hardy was on his feet rushing the dazed guard who had been struck by the opening door. He was vaguely familiar, a big red-haired ranny, with his nose bleeding and a glassy look in his eyes as he tried to lift the six-gun he held. Drew swept it aside casually with his left hand, slammed the barrel of his own Colt against the side of the man's head. He dropped to his knees, swaying, and Drew placed a boot against his chest and kicked him flat to the floor where he lay still.

Whirling at a sound behind him, Drew held his fire as he recognized Denny Clarke, a valise in hand, tippy-toeing towards the door. The lawyer had a white ridged line of fear outlining his lips, face like chalk.

'Don't go yet, Denny,' Drew told him and the lawyer flattened himself against the wall, dropped his valise as he thrust his hands shoulder-high.

'Don't shoot me!'

'I ought to, you damn snake — all the trouble you've caused. Get back in your office.' Drew stooped and picked up the valise as Clarke sidled along the wall to the narrow door leading into his main office. He went in quickly, Drew following, glancing at the two body-guards. The redhead was out on the floor to one side of the sagging door.

The shot man was huddled in a corner, groaning but barely conscious.

Drew kicked the door closed, noted that the little damage done by the fire had been repaired or painted over. He crossed the room so he could watch the door as well as Denny Clarke, who had dropped into his desk chair and was mopping his face with a kerchief. 'I knew you'd be back.'

Drew dropped the valise on the desk. 'Open it.'

Denny seemed about to speak but fumbled with the catches and opened the valise. Drew moved the gun barrel and the lawyer swallowed, upended the valise and spilled papers on to the desk. Drew frowned.

'Which one is Emmett's will?'

Denny Clarke licked his lips, tried to hold Drew's hard gaze but couldn't, lowered his eyes. 'Not there — actually.'

'Then where is it — actually?'

Denny sat back in his chair, breathing hard and fast now. 'Drew — it-it's my only ace-in-the-hole. You're hell on wheels an' — I–I knew you'd come in like cavalry in full charge. I — gotta have somethin' to bargain with!'

Drew leaned forward swiftly and whipped the Colt's foresight across Clarke's face. The man screamed and reared back, blood streaming. He dabbed frantically at it with his kerchief.

'Ain't in a bargaining mood. You produce that will in the next two minutes, or you're gonna be followed by every pariah dog in Hangtree trying to get at the raw meat that'll be your face — I'm running against the clock, Denny.'

Clarke stared up at him, holding the kerchief against the cut cheek, eyes bright with his fear. 'Drew — there's a new West Texas Railroad Company wanting to link El Paso and Van Horn, through Sierra Blanca. They need to cross Lazy H land and they're willing to pay almost anything for the rights . . .

'Your time's running out, Denny.'

'Drew! For Chris'sakes, man — Lazy

H has more than enough land to run the herds you boys have.'

'Kerry and Luke have,' Drew corrected him coldly. 'You saw to that. But it doesn't matter . . . I want that will.'

Still Denny tried to argue or cajole and Drew grabbed the front of his shirt and hauled him halfway across the desk, Colt barrel moving towards the good side of his face. The lawyer screamed and one hand came out of the top desk drawer with a short-barrelled Sheriff's model Smith & Wesson revolver.

Drew twisted away as it blasted and he felt the heat of its passage past his face. He slammed the Colt across Clarke's head as the man fired again, but this time the bullet splintered a corner of the desk before the gun thudded to the floor. Drew heaved Denny into a corner where he sagged, eyes crossed, blood running from under his hairline.

He was dazed but snapped his eyes open quickly as Drew pressed the gun muzzle next to his ear.

'I fire this alongside your ear, it'll burst the drum. Then I'll do the other one. You'll be deaf, Denny, and if you think that's a lot of fun, you got a surprise coming — but that's only for starters. I don't have a lot of time so I have to be kind of crude — and I guess I learned a lot of crude in Hudspeth. You've no idea some of the animals they have there. Fact, it's an insult to animals to call 'em that.'

'Aw, Drew! So much money! Can't we deal . . . ?' He stiffened as the gun hammer cocked back alongside his ear. 'OK, OK! Damn you! I-I'll get the blasted will — and to hell with you!'

Muttering constantly Denny Clarke knelt beside a tall, narrow filing cabinet. Drew was surprised at how easily he tilted it back after releasing some hidden catch. It must have been counterbalanced to a nicety and revealed a dark, square hole underneath. Denny reluctantly reached into the hidey-hole.

And Drew lunged towards him as the man made his last desperate move, brought out another gun. He fired too soon and the flash lit the interior of the hole, splintered the floor boards. But Drew had reacted instinctively and his bullet punched Denny into a corner where he lay on one side, face slack, blood on his shirt front.

Drew pushed him out of the way, reached into the hole and brought out a document tied with pink lawyers' tape. He recognized Emmett's handwriting on one side.

Last will and testament
of
Emmett Drew Hardy

Drew Hardy almost jumped out of his skin as he reached the bottom of the outside stairway and turned into the lane on his way to his horse, the will tucked inside his shirt.

What made him jump was Pop Cansdale stepping out of a side doorway of the druggist's, holding a sawn-off shotgun.

'Reckoned it'd be you makin' all that ruckus, Drew. Now you go easy, boy. I ain't used one of these in a lot of years, but even with my rheumatics I can still pull a mean trigger.'

Drew lifted his hands slightly away from his sides, smiled faintly. 'I won't give you any argument, Pop.'

Cansdale grunted, face wrinkled like a beach at low tide. He saw the edge of the legal papers poking out of Drew's shirt. 'Hah! You got Emmett's will I reckon — been talk about it round town. No one b'lieved he'd cut you out, Drew. Had to be a forgery.'

'This is the real one, Pop. I haven't read it yet.'

Cansdale sniffed, jerked the shotgun slightly towards the upstairs office. 'Guess Denny din' wanta hand it over.'

'He was — reluctant.'

Pop Cansdale laughed, a cackle that brought on a cough that shook the frail old body. Drew pushed the shotgun down without effort, and Cansdale tucked the weapon under one arm while he fumbled out a handkerchief, coughed into it. Wheezing, he said, 'You had it rough, boy. An' I long ago forgave you for all that cheek you an' Matt Dekker used to gimme when I was takin' my — cough medicine. Always made me kinda stagger that medicine . . . '

Drew smiled. 'We noticed. Thanks, Pop. Reckon you can handle Roy?'

'Cripes, boy, I ain't *that* old!'

There had been folk gathering, no doubt wondering about the gunfire — and seeing the strange sight of Pop Cansdale hurrying along with a sawed-off shotgun. But the bunched people suddenly scattered and Drew tensed, hearing galloping horses.

Two riders skidded their mounts across the entrance to the lane and Drew had his second shock since leaving Denny Clarke's office.

Lee Dekker, dishevelled and dusty from a hard ride, dismounted and hurried towards him. Behind her was a worried-looking Shelby Goddard.

'Oh, Drew!' the girl said breathlessly as she stopped before him. 'Shelby here — rescued me from Lazy H. From Luke really — he got drunk and — amorous. They were holding me in a disused root cellar with rats and snakes.' She shuddered, gulped, and as the crowd closed around a little more, young Goddard came up looking sheepish.

Lee smiled wearily and took his arm. 'This is my rescuer, Drew. He knocked Luke out — with a flatiron!'

The crowd murmured at that and Shelby blushed some but there was a sly, pleased smile on his face, too.

'Good work, kid.'

'I-I might've killed him,' Goddard admitted worriedly, 'I was kinda riled.'

'Luke's always had a hard head — ' Drew took the will from inside his shirt. 'This is Emmett's original last will and testament.' Then he had a sudden thought. 'What about Kerry? You see him?'

'We saw dust heading towards Lazy

H. Shelby brought us out by another trail, away from the usual one. It could have been Kerry making that dust.'

Drew frowned, looked at Goddard. 'Is Lazy H being worked by a bunch of hardcases, these days?'

'Well, Luke and Kerry have their own crew, half a dozen hardcases they use when they need 'em. The rest are regular cowboys, some from your time — and a lot of 'em are worried about what Kerry and Luke are doin' to the spread — and you.' He shifted weight from one foot to the other. 'Lots of bunkhouse gossip, you know, but it ain't all wild talk.'

Lee squeezed Drew's arm. 'That's good to know. You'll have a loyal crew when you take over what's rightfully yours, Drew.'

'Well, I ain't read this will yet.'

Lee took it from him and immediately identified it as the original document she had seen when working for Denny Clarke.

'This was the one where he left Lazy

H to all three of you, Drew, equally divided. But Kerry and Luke thought they could share the ranch between them by having Denny fake another will. With you still in jail . . . '

Drew had been unfolding the document and reading it while Lee was talking. He glanced up, nodding.

'Yeah — Emmett left Lazy H to be divided equally between the three of us. Denny told Kerry and Luke I'd been left half, while they had only a quarter share each. He never showed them the will itself and he knew they'd be riled and easily agreed when he suggested faking a new one that cut me out completely.'

'I don't think he would have had to work very hard to have your brothers agree to that anyway, Drew. Not after the way they treated you over the years.'

Drew glanced at her sharply. 'I was working for Denny at the time, remember. I saw and heard almost everything that went on between Kerry and Luke and Denny — and then I had

226

to type it all up. They were always going to cheat you out of a share of Lazy H, Drew . . . I'm sorry, but — '

He folded the document and handed it to her. 'Will you hold on to this, Lee? I think I'm going to have to ride out to Lazy H and I'd like to know Emmett's will is safe.'

'Can't you wait for the sheriff to come back, Drew?'

He smiled thinly. 'Roy Tierney's got no love for any of the Hardys. He'd love to see a full-blown feud between us all.'

She frowned, obviously concerned. 'Drew, I believe they intend to kill you.'

He nodded. 'Reckon so. They always were mean sonofas. But this has to be settled, Lee. Now's the time to do it.'

'Will-will you try to do some kind of deal with them?'

He hesitated, shook his head. 'Way past that. Reckon it always has been.'

'But you can't ride out there and face them! You heard Shell say they have half-a-dozen hardcases to back them . . .'

'Lee.'

Both looked up as Shelby Goddard spoke her name. He was pointing past the edge of the crowd to a rider coming into Main, raising a long dust cloud.

Drew recognized Kerry right away, turned and jumped for Shelby Goddard's horse. He swung into leather and the crowd scattered again as he spurred out into Main where Kerry could see him. He halted Goddard's buckskin and it pranced a little with the unfamiliar rider, but Drew was concentrating on Kerry.

His brother skidded his sweating mount to a halt about ten yards away, face grim beneath its mask of dust. Kerry's wild eyes seemed to blaze in his face as he raked them over the crowd, picked out Lee and Shelby Goddard. He flicked his gaze to Drew.

'God*damn* you, Drew! You ain't gonna win! I won't let you!'

'Hold up a minute, Kerry!' Drew said but his brother was already raking his hard-ridden mount with his spurs. The horse whinnied but responded, leaping forward and charging Drew where he sat the buckskin. Kerry's six-gun came up and he triggered wildly. Rage and the motion of the charging horse threw his aim wild, but he kept shooting.

Drew wrenched the buckskin's reins, lying along its neck as Kerry's bullets whipped overhead. He palmed up his own six-gun — but he was too late.

There was wild whinnying and whistling from the horses as they collided, both animals trying to rear aside, eyes rolling, bodies twisting, the occasional hoof striking out. Drew felt the buckskin going down under him, kicked his boots free of the stirrups but didn't have time to jump clear. He hit hard and the buckskin, almost on its back, rolled across his legs, its own legs thrashing. The big body convulsed as it tried to get up but Kerry's mount's weight held it. And the Lazy H horse was doing plenty of kicking and snapping and writhing in an effort to free itself from the tangle.

Drew was flung free, rolled away in

the dust, losing his Colt somewhere in the process. Dazed, half-blinded by dust, he sat up, crab-crawled out of the way as the horses finally lunged to their feet. Both ran across his vision in the same direction.

Kerry was revealed then, half on his feet, looking around desperately for his six-gun.

Drew lowered his head and charged. He hit his brother hard in the body and everyone heard Kerry's loud gusting of air being smashed from his lungs as Drew's weight carried them both over into the dust again.

They rolled and elbowed and kneed and kicked. Kerry even tried to bite Drew's right ear but caught an elbow under the left eye that made him desist hurriedly. They burst away from each other, both on hands and knees, thrusting up, blood and dust streaking their faces.

Neither of them was even aware of the crowd now, the men cheering, the womenfolk trying to drag them away, some already hurrying home with a couple of kids who had been with them.

They rushed in, bodies jarring as they met. Kerry started swinging but Drew changed tactics, ducked under Kerry's arm, grabbed the wrist as it came over his shoulder and straightened, roaring aloud with the effort as he lifted his brother clear off his feet. He grunted again as he heaved Kerry over his head and the older Hardy hit the dust and skidded, the wind knocked out of him.

Face scarred by the gravel, pressed against the street, he gasped for breath, little puffs of dust rising with each exhalation, blinking, hands pressing into the ground. His body tensed as he prepared to lift up and Drew stepped in, kicked him sharply in the side. Kerry rolled away, gagging, and as he flopped on to his face, he saw a six-gun not three feet away, half buried in the dust.

He didn't know whether it was his own Colt or Drew's. Nor did he care.

Now he would end this once and for all!

He snatched the gun up as he rolled over it, brought it around in both hands and levelled it at Drew who froze in the midst of a forward lunge, stumbling.

Drew knew he was dead.

Kerry was a good shot, even now, shaking with exertion and hate.

Drew crouched, wondering which way to dive, knowing it would only be a desperation move, anyway. The gun barked and he felt the bullet take him in the side, spinning him so that he floundered before falling.

He glimpsed Kerry through a red haze, teeth bared now in triumph as he took a staggering step closer, gun cocked, steadied in both dirt-smeared hands, lining the barrel up with Drew's head.

Then there was the thundering roar of a shotgun and Kerry was hurled back, smashed off his feet, doubled over. His broken body hit the dust, skidded and came to a halt, blood smearing the street's surface.

Blinking, Drew pressed a hand into his wounded side, looking around — in time to see Pop Cansdale spit a stream of tobacco juice as he lowered his shotgun with its two smoking barrels.

'Told you I hadn't lost me touch,' Pop said proudly.

★ ★ ★

Luke Hardy took three days to come out of his coma.

Shelby Goddard was worried as all get-out that he was going to die but, like Drew had said, Luke had a hard head. He recovered from the severe concussion, but his left eye was bandaged, giving him a lop-sided look.

His one good eye glared coldly at Drew who was walking with the aid of a stick, due to the bullet creasing his side, again on the left. Drew sat on the end of the bed.

'God damn you, Drew! Doc says I'll likely lose the sight in one eye! Thanks to your bullet kickin' rock chips into it.'

'Lucky the bullet didn't hit *you*.'

Luke glared more intensely. 'So — you won after all, you son of a bitch!'

Drew spread his hands, had to catch his falling walking stick he had forgotten about. 'Won what? Emmett's will left the spread to you, Kerry and me. Equal shares. Kerry's dead so it reverts to just you and me now.'

Luke snorted. 'You think I want to share the spread with you! Like hell! Now with only one eye . . . Jesus Christ, I've hated you all my life and I don't feel one bit different now! Fact is, if I had a gun, I'd kill you where you stand.'

'You always was a sore loser, Luke. You don't want to share, so what do you want to do? Build a fence down the middle, you stay on your side, me on mine?'

'Ah no! I've thought about this. *You buy me out*!'

Drew hadn't expected that and was silent for a short time.. 'Can't do that, Luke, and you know it.'

'Know nothin' of the sort.' He bared his teeth in a cold tight smile, his single eye glinting. 'All you gotta do is borrow agin your half — a big fat mortgage that'll take you the rest of your life to pay off!' He laughed shortly. 'Hey! Mebbe I was wrong about you winnin' after all!'

'Only one answer to that, Luke. No, I don't aim to go into debt for you or anyone else.'

Luke's scabbed face straightened, his jaw jutting. 'Well, you better damn well do somethin'! 'Cause I ain't sharin' the spread with you.'

'You want to buy *me* out?'

Luke blinked. 'Ah, no you don't! *I* ain't tyin' myself up with any mortgage!'

Drew nodded. 'OK. How about this? You take, as your share, the land the West Texas Railroad's interested in. Sell it to 'em, and I'll keep the rest of the spread.'

Luke snorted. 'Oh, sure! And that'll give you a lot more'n half of Lazy H.'

'Yeah, but the railroad'll pay a

premium to get that land, a lot more than if you just tried to sell your half of Lazy H. According to Denny Clarke, they've had one setback already and had to pull out. Now they've got a second chance and need it bad — otherwise, it means tunnelling through the ranges and they don't have the time nor money for that.'

Luke's frown stayed in place as he gave Drew's suggestion some deep thought. His lips moved as he juggled sums of money in his head, figuring how much he could stick the railroad for. They were over a barrel and, like Drew said, he could get a lot more than if he tried to sell off his half of Lazy H — *a lot more* . . .

His face was as deadpan as it could be under the scabs and the slanted bandage. 'Might work out. I'll let you know.'

That was good enough for Drew. Luke already knew he had no choice but wouldn't admit it out loud. 'Don't leave it too long, Luke.'

'Don't you order me around, you son of a bitch!'

Drew pretended to shoot him wih thumb and forefinger, nodded curtly and left the infirmary.

Lee Dekker was waiting outside in the Lazy H buckboard. She held his walking stick as he clambered aboard and settled beside her.

'What's Luke going to do?'

'Get rich quick — he hopes. I hope, too.' He told her briefly about his suggestion. 'Sooner he moves out of Hangtree the better.'

She looked at him steadily. 'Yes, I agree . . . well, where to? Home to Lazy H . . .?'

He looked at her sharply, smiled slowly. 'That 'home' has a nice sound to it — specially if you're thinking of making it your home too.'

'Well, that's kind of up to you, isn't it?'

He hitched a little closer. 'And a parson.'

'Let's see if we can find one,' she said, laughing, as she lifted the reins and started the buckboard moving.

We do hope that you have enjoyed reading this large print book.

Did you know that all of our titles are available for purchase?

We publish a wide range of high quality large print books including:
Romances, Mysteries, Classics
General Fiction
Non Fiction and Westerns

Special interest titles available in large print are:
The Little Oxford Dictionary
Music Book, Song Book
Hymn Book, Service Book

Also available from us courtesy of Oxford University Press:
Young Readers' Dictionary
(large print edition)
Young Readers' Thesaurus
(large print edition)

For further information or a free brochure, please contact us at:
Ulverscroft Large Print Books Ltd.,
The Green, Bradgate Road, Anstey,
Leicester, LE7 7FU, England.
Tel: (00 44) 0116 236 4325
Fax: (00 44) 0116 234 0205

Other titles in the
Linford Western Library:

THE LAST GUNDOWN

Matt James

A town without mercy, a land without heart or soul: that was what bounty hunter Shell Dunbar confronted during that endless blazing summer. Even the handful of men who supported him gave him no chance of surviving that murderous summer of hate. They had already given him up for dead when he faced the last gundown . . .

DEATH RIDER

Boyd Cassidy

Mountain man Rufas Kane discovers Dan Cooper's dead body on a hillside overlooking the town of Death, leaving the townsfolk wondering why anyone would kill a harmless cowboy. Then one of Gene Adams' cowboys is killed in a gunfight with the ruthless Trey Skinner. It becomes apparent that Skinner is responsible for Cooper's death. But nothing's as it seems. That night, amid a spate of killings, Gene Adams vows to find the killer before dawn, or to die trying.

BIG TROUBLE AT FLAT ROCK

Elliot Long

Callum Bowden stared down at his adoptive father, John McKendry, lying dead in his coffin. He could barely look at the lifeless face and the silk wrapping that covered the ghastly wound across the throat ... Meanwhile, hatred had overwhelmed Jim McKendry, who swore that someone would pay for his father's death: no matter what it took, the killer would be brought to justice — alive or dead.

RANGELAND JUSTICE

Rob Hill

Jack Just, weary from long days on the trail, rides into an isolated cattle town on the Texas panhandle. There he finds that the greedy and powerful Clovis Blacklake has the town in his pocket. But when Jack also discovers that Blacklake has cheated the town's most downtrodden inhabitant out of his rightful property, he decides to make a stand. It takes a real man to fight the ruthless Blacklake; and when Jack does, the tables begin to turn . . .